Abra

Book 2 in the Galaxy Sanctuary Alien Abduction Romance
Series
By
Alana Khan

Copyright

Acknowledgments

I want to thank my daughter, Amarra Skye, an author in her own right, who always has great ideas when I plot myself into a corner.

Also thanks to Dr. Lee who started as an early reader and has become my revered Development Editor because of her terrific insights and helpful suggestions. Our relationship is certainly a bonus I never imagined when I started my writing journey.

Of course, I have to acknowledge Stephanie A. from across the pond who tirelessly works on my behalf and eagerly reads my books before their first edit. Hopefully she will someday learn that favorite doesn't have a 'u' and dates start with the month, not the date. I appreciate her despite these little flaws!

I have alpha and beta teams who read my books before they are ready for prime time. They help me fix plot holes and typos, make my heroes more heroic, and ensure my heroines are never too stupid to live.

Thanks to the following people for all their input: Anne-Marie S., Shardae M., Shannon B., Danielle M., Lorraine B., Naomi B., Kimberly F., Betty R., Anuschka-Marie W., Corda A., Kathleen F., Kimber J., Kaye S., and Christine R.

Would you like to join my team? To become an early reader contact me at alankhanauthor@gmail.com

Want my FREE newsletter with all things Khan and the Alanaverse? Cover reveals, giveaways, early free chapters? And did I mention contests? Like suggest another name for the p**** word (winner: *xizca*) or get to name one of my characters (several winners including Dawn the heroine in Book 3 of this series). You'll also get your choice of a FREE BOOK when you sign up.

Present Day
On Planet Fairea

Chapter One

Abraxx

I shouldn't be here. I should have known better than to try to have fun.

Having fun, that's an interesting condition to aspire to for a male who was recently freed after long *lunars* in an underground dungeon. At least I'm walking on my own two feet. When our liberators found us, we all had to be carried out. I guess that's what being fed sporadic rations and not allowed to see the sun for *lunars* at a time will do to you.

When I decided to visit the fair, I thought I deserved it. Thought I deserved a moment's happiness after what I've endured since I was abducted from my home planet of Numa fifteen *annums* ago. It was a bad decision.

I stalk through the fairgrounds watching the people like I used to watch the bugs back on Numa, with a vague interest but no real attachment. I doubt I'll ever shake this feeling of not belonging, even though everyone back at Sanctuary calls us a family.

Dawn is right when she calls us a big, dysfunctional family. What do you expect when you have ten different species learning to live together? One is even a male who can shift into a bestial canine. Add to that the fact we've all been enslaved and mistreated, and you have a unique combination of grim unhappiness laced with slivers of hope.

Aimlessly following one dirt path after another, I pass the food booth area. There are dishes here from half the known galaxy. The smell of spitted meat should make my mouth water, but I find myself not very hungry since I was freed three weeks ago. It doesn't make sense. You'd think after being underground and given only the minimal amount to eat for *lunars,* I'd be gorging myself morning and evening, but food lacks appeal. That's not surprising. Everything lacks appeal.

Shadows are lengthening. Dusk is a long affair on planet Fairea, what with its three suns. They travel at odd trajectories to each other, but they all seem to set around the same time each night.

Someone's playing a stringed instrument and singing on my right; the sound of native drums drifts through the air on my left. I used to love music back on Numa. When my parents played, I danced with abandon. Those days seem like a vid now. Like I'm watching someone else's life.

Stolen by slavers at age eighteen, brought to a *ludus,* a gladiator training school, and taught to fight, I was a middle-tier gladiator who fought well enough to stay alive. I never strived to become one of the greats. Looking back, I wonder if even then part of me wanted to die. For some reason, I kept fighting so I could keep breathing and walking upright.

When I lost three matches in a row, my owner, Daneur Khour, brought me to his compound on Fairea and threw me into an underground dungeon with other gladiators he accused of 'underperforming'. As the head of the MarZan cartel, Khour was one of the most powerful crime bosses in the galaxy.

The guards would occasionally pull us from our cells, haul us into the bright sunlight that burned our eyes, and beat or kill us. Vids of this treatment were beamed to his fighting flesh all over the galaxy and used as motivation. By the time we were rescued, there were eight of us holding onto life by a thread.

Shaking my head to force those images out of my mind, I wonder what I was thinking. That I could come to the fair and the last fifteen *annums* would fall away? Disappear? That I could just lose myself in the crowd and have fun? I should return to my hover and go back to the compound.

"Come one, come all," drifts to me from the path up ahead. "The show starts in just a few *minimas*. You will see a dancing female who is so beautiful she will haunt your dreams for years to come. Then I'll tell you about the most remarkable product ever manufactured on this or any other planet.

"Come on in. The show's about to begin. I won't even try to part you from your hard-earned credits. I just want to give you a free show."

The crowd in the dirt walkway surges around me, dragging me toward the barker. I recall traveling with my family to a fair on Numa. As a child, I was fascinated by shows like this, by the barkers and the promise of magical cures and potions. I wonder if this will be the same as I remember from those days when I was safe and naïve and loved.

A whiff of damp soil wafts into my nose, and suddenly I'm back in that underground cell. I held out hope for a long time. I paced and exercised and tried to keep my body strong despite the infrequent feedings. After all, how long could they keep expensive fighting flesh locked in a windowless dungeon?

As it turned out, they did it for a long time. I lost hope slowly over days and weeks and *lunars*. I quit exercising partly because I was demoralized, partly because I didn't have the energy to do more than sit on my bunk.

One day I didn't sit up at all. I just laid there. That day turned into many. After being ravenous for so long, I had no desire for food. I became despondent just like every other male in that hole in the ground. It wasn't long after that I decided I wanted death. I began to fixate on it.

I died in that cell *lunar* cycles ago. My body just never got the message.

I was warned that if I didn't eat my rations or drink the water allotted to me then not only me but every comrade in the other cells would be flogged. None of us could let that happen, so we all ate and drank our meager rations and just waited for the day when it was our turn to be pulled into the harsh sunlight and executed. Khour's reputation for sadistic pleasure had been well earned.

A few weeks ago, a band of gladiators on a mission to kill Khour came to the compound where we were being held. For different reasons and in different ways, he was making their life hell, too. They killed the bastard and freed us all. We were so debilitated we had to be carried out of that pit of despair and nursed back to health.

Papers were forged and the gladiators gave seed money to the eight males and five human female slaves they liberated that day. Bayne, the canine shifter, and his human mate Willa were part of the team that rescued us. They chose to stay here. I think it's so he can run in the forest and meadows.

Now we're trying to build lives for ourselves in the very compound where we were held prisoner. There is something truly liberating in turning our place of confinement and horror into a sanctuary.

"Watch where you're going," a deep male voice bellows as he jostles me from behind and jolts me from the imagined darkness of the dungeon back to reality. I don't curse at him; I'm the one who halted in the middle of a busy pathway.

The barker yells, "Step on up," then puts a small stringed instrument under his whiskered chin and plays it with a bow. It's a lively tune designed to catch a casual passerby's interest.

Planet Fairea is a vacation destination because of this fair. It has grown over the centuries and now covers thousands of *rextans* of land. People come from all over the galaxy to enjoy the fairgrounds and sample the wares.

They've kept it looking like it was when they began it so long ago. It still has dirt pathways and old-fashioned booths made of wood and emblazoned with fabric. Now fairgoers are given computer pads to find their way through the complicated maze of pathways, but other technological advances are shunned. Once you leave your hover in the lot, you can imagine you've stepped back in time.

People are encouraged to wear the garb of their ancestors when they visit. Most do. I see females in elaborate ankle-length gowns, some with long flowing veils or feathered hats. Some males are wearing antique uniforms or other costumes from bygone days in their culture.

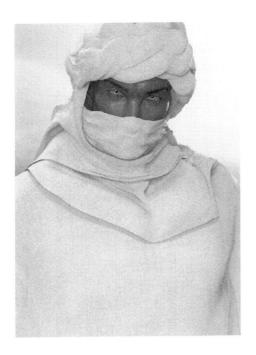

I'm wearing my long *sha'rill*, a thin blue fabric I drape around my body to cover me from head to toe. Only my eyes show. It's the garment my people have worn for centuries to keep them cool in the heat of summer. Since our liberation it's what I wear every day. It keeps me hidden, which allows me to feel partially invisible even in this throng of aliens.

I'm used to trying to stay hidden. I'm humanoid, but others say my *brill*, the thick ropes of flesh on my head where most other species have hair, is disturbing.

My feet carry me to the booth with the barker who is now playing his instrument with abandon. I'm not interested in watching this show and hearing about whatever product he's shilling, but I'm still partially back in that dungeon. I'll wait here until I shake off the black memories that accompany the urge to quit eating and allow myself to die.

The last of the three suns sets as the barker places his foot on a wooden stool, his bow sawing lightning-quick against the strings.

"Welcome females and males," he says after he stops playing and allows the instrument to dangle from his fingers. "I'm Enoch. Let me introduce the incomparable Juno who will dance for you," his voice is deep and gruff.

A female enters from behind the wagon in which it appears the two live. Although the barker is an old, bearded Thracian, the female is young. She looks Morganian or human; I can't tell their species apart.

She steps to the front of the open circle where a white substance on the ground marks off the area. It's lit with eight-*fierto* flaming torches. The way she moves commands attention. Each rise and fall of her feet is graceful and lithe.

Her skirt is made of colorful cloth strips of varying lengths. When she moves, they sway and float in the breeze almost as if they have a life of their own.

Her midriff is bare, and her breasts are covered in stretchy material of iridescent green. It sparkles almost as if it's made of jewels.

My fingers ache to trace the soft curve of exposed flesh that travels between the two garments. My nostrils are no longer filled with the smell of the humid depths of my underground cell, they're flared to catch a whiff of her scent.

When Enoch plays, Juno dances, following the music, eyes cast down. Her movements are perfection, arms graceful, fingers curved to look natural. Everything about her could be drawn to illustrate a book about elegance.

Desire blooms in the center of my chest as I'm mesmerized by the hypnotic swivel of her hips, the artful toss of her head, the lovely symmetry of her features.

Yet her face is impassive. There is no joy. All it takes is one look at her long, delicate neck to see what the problem is. She wears a slave collar.

Masters can force slaves to perform, to work, to dance. They even compelled me to risk my life. But we can't be ordered to be happy.

Her form is beautiful, though. Mesmerizing. I watch as the music's pace increases, becomes more frenzied. Her steps grow livelier until she leaps and soars. I could stand here and watch her for *hoaras*.

During one of her jumps, her eyes catch mine. She almost stumbles on her landing. Now as she dances, her gaze remains locked on me. Each time she twirls, her glance catches mine when she faces forward again, as if she's anchoring herself to me.

When her pink tongue slides between her lips, my cock believes the gesture was meant for him. I haven't been hard in an *annum*. In the dungeon, I was too debilitated to waste the energy, and my mind had no desire to yearn for something it couldn't have.

I've been free for weeks and my cock has yet to reassert himself. I assumed many parts of me died in that cell, and sexual desire was one of those things. Yet I feel it now.

I feel alive for the first time in *annums*. Fully alive. It's as though I can feel the blood pumping in my veins and my heart beating in my chest. Desire and attraction sail through me. Can she see it in my eyes, I wonder, because I see it in hers.

Where before her expression was dead, now her eyes are sparked with interest. Although I'm in the rear of the crowd, my height puts me a head taller than everyone in front of me, so her gaze unerringly finds me again and again. There are over a hundred people crammed into this small semi-circle, but for the briefest moment, it's as if it's just the two of us—Juno and me.

She leaves her position of safety near the old-fashioned covered wagon and moves through the crowd. At first, the people refused to let her through, but when it became clear she was leaving her makeshift stage, a space opened in front of her as if it were choreographed.

She's still whirling and dancing, but she's making her way through the throng. Directly toward me. At the start, she looked around her, making eye contact with others, but now she's making no pretense of being interested in anyone but me.

I hold her gaze, my eyes never veering from hers, as I silently will her to approach. I have no need to smile, although she can't see me through my *sha'rill*, there's nothing funny about this. No, this attraction feels serious, weighty.

Come closer, I tell her with my thoughts, my gaze, my body.

Nothing can stop me, she seems to respond.

When she's two *fiertos* away, her hand gracefully arches toward me in silent invitation to grasp it. Grasp it, I do.

Turning from me, my hand still in her grip, she hurries back to her original dancing area as she tugs my unresisting body behind her. She releases my hand, spins toward me and dances. The look in her eyes and the hint of a smile on her beautiful lips encourage me to join her.

A silent voice in the back of my mind wants to protest, to tell her I don't dance, but my body doesn't get the message. I dance with the abandon I had as a youngling and the grace I acquired after *annums* of training in the *ludus*.

My hips gyrate, my feet stomp, my shoulders sway, even my tail is raised, slashing in time with the music. For the first time in decades, I'm one with the music. It's as if an old machine, rusty for years, received desperately needed oil.

Every cell of my body is alive and moving and feeling free for the first time since those slavers stole me so many *annums* ago. My face feels odd until I realize I'm smiling. My muscles haven't pulled into this configuration in a very long time.

Look at her. She's more beautiful up close than she was from my position at the back of the audience. Since she wears no cosmetics, I couldn't see from afar what I see now—the delicate bow of her pink lips, the elegant line of her nose, or those brown eyes that appear so deep you could dive into them.

Enoch quickens the music's pace and Juno and I are dancing and lifting our feet in perfect sync with each other. After she twirls, her gaze always searches for mine when she faces me again. When she does, she grants me the tiniest of smiles each time.

I don't understand this, but we have a connection. It's wordless and silent as the depths of space and yet somehow deep as the ocean.

The music slows, then stops. The barker gives the crowd scant moments to applaud, then begins his pitch.

Juno has been dismissed, but instead of boarding the crude wooden wagon, she places her back to it, cocks a leg to brace her foot against it, and silently beckons me to stand next to her.

I've been living with six human females since I was freed from the dungeon. I've gotten used to their foreign features. This one is beautiful. Her hair flows in long golden-brown waves that hang almost to her waist. Her eyes are shaped like oval *tiffong* leaves and tilt up at the edges. Her nose is pert and for some reason, I would describe it as regal. And her lips. Her lips are pink and plump and perfect.

The fact that I want to kiss them shocks me. But it's a fact, nonetheless.

I tune in to the barker for a moment, just to see what he's selling and for Juno and me to catch our breath. He's extolling the virtues of some potion designed to cure everything from diarrhea to warts. Juno's job is to pull in the crowds. His is to make them part with their hard-earned credits.

I'm a tall male. Tall and strong—at least I used to be. That's why I was abducted from Numa and forced to fight as a gladiator. Since my appetite hasn't returned, I've forced myself to eat the highly nutritious meals the cooks have prepared to help us regain our strength.

The medic has formulated a special daily tonic, unique for each of us, to improve our nutrition and speed our recovery. I've also pushed myself to slowly increase my exercise routines in the *ludus*. Although I'm still a shadow of what I used to be, a great deal of my muscle tone and strength has returned. I'm glad of it now because no matter how many people jostle me from behind, I remain standing next to Juno.

Juno

What is it about the Numan, I wonder. I look up at him and take his measure. I want to discover what's so special about him, why he's caught my interest. In the years I've been forced to dance for Enoch, I've never pulled anyone out of the audience to dance with me. It was like I was drawn toward him by an unseen force.

My heart is racing. I haven't felt hopeful or eager or optimistic since the slave collar was fastened around my neck six years ago. But I feel it now. It's like the air is charged with lightning. Dancing with the Numan was exhilarating. We were in perfect step with each other. Always in sync.

There was a moment on the makeshift stage when he reached out and touched my hand. It was the most innocent touch. I don't think it was premeditated. He was just dancing with such abandon and it felt so right for us to make physical contact—to connect. I felt the oddest explosion in my chest. It was like fireworks, or maybe an incendiary bomb. I can't figure it out, it was so brief, yet so compelling.

I danced my best. I always do. Before, it was always to avoid Enoch's wrath. Tonight? Tonight was to please the Numan.

Numans aren't rare, I've seen them before. I've seen lots of species in the six years I've been in space. Sometimes I feel like I've seen it all. Jaded. At twenty-four I've seen far too much.

I've been through three owners and countless trauma. At last count I've traveled to seven planets. I've been used for serving and servicing and now I'm forced to dance. Although this is the best of all my jobs as a slave, I'm still a slave. It's a lucky break that Enoch's cock barely works, and when he uses it, he prefers boys.

I can't contain the rueful laugh that escapes my lips. Yeah, this is a dream job alright. I don't get raped by my owner and I get to dance. Lucky me. I still wear the cold metal pain/kill collar around my neck. My life isn't my own.

The Numan is watching me. It's not like every other man in the crowd who examines me up and down as if they're deciding which hole they'd like to stick their cock into. The Numan seems to like looking at my face. I like looking at his, too—what I can see of it, that is.

He has a proud bearing. Shoulders back, head held high, intelligent eyes. His body is fit, even though it's hard to tell under the blue muslin robe he's wearing. When he danced, he moved with such masculine grace I found it hard to tear my eyes from him. Even his tail, peeking out from under his robe, moved with elegance.

I've always wondered what the things on Numan's heads feel like. They're like plump tentacles of flesh that cascade off their scalp instead of hair. I can't see his, but I can see their form under the fabric of his garb.

He's not interested in what Enoch's selling, which is a testament to his intellect. And he's not moving on, which is a testament to the fact that he's interested in me. I finger my collar, giving him a hint, reminding him his interest will be wasted. At least I hope it will be. Sometimes when credits are low, Enoch accepts offers from males who want to buy something other than the snake oil he sells.

He doesn't step in the back of the line, though, which is what that type of male does. He's content to stand next to me. He's looking at me with eyes that are aqua-blue. And kind. I can't see his mouth, but by his eyes I'm certain he's smiling at me.

"Hello," his voice is deep. I can't quite put my finger on why I immediately decide his voice also sounds kind.

"I'm Abraxx, from Numa. Thank you for the dance. It was . . . a rare gift. May I speak with you, Juno?"

Surprising. The males who want me don't usually introduce themselves. They never ask for what they want, they just talk to Enoch about an exchange of goods and services, then take what they've paid for. And they never, ever remember my name.

In the beginning I tried to fight, to refuse to give what was demanded of me. The painful lesson of the shock collar taught me resistance is futile. So I've learned to disconnect my mind while my body performs as ordered. I know instinctively that's not what Abraxx from Numa is after—at least I hope not.

"Yes, we can talk."

I look up at him; he's even taller than I'd thought. His garb covers a lot, but it can't hide the kind masculine energy rolling off him in waves.

"You dance like a dream."

My gaze darts to the dirt between us and I chuckle with embarrassment. Like a dream, huh? My ballet teacher back in Creve Coeur, Missouri wouldn't have said that. She would have scolded me for not arching my back enough or having the proper turnout of my feet.

"Thanks." It's been a long time since I've heard a compliment of any kind. It ignites a spark deep in my chest.

"How long have you worn a slave collar?"

The question would be abrasive from someone else, but there's something about the kindness in his eyes and his gentle tone that prevents it from being provocative.

"Six years. Six years since I was abducted."

My stomach makes its hunger known with one loud growl, then another.

"When was the last time you ate?"

"Yesterday."

"Can I get you some food?"

Is he offering me food? Really? Our wagon is close enough to the food booths for me to be tempted by delicious smells from morning to night. My master is too cheap to buy me anything fresh. Every other day I get something stale or almost rotten.

"What's your favorite thing to eat at the fair?" he asks, his head cocked at an appealing angle.

"The *revensell* looks delicious." I've watched people walking by with huge hunks of spitted meat. They're as big as the brontosaurus leg hanging off Fred Flintstone's car and smell like the best barbecue from back home. "I've never tried it, though."

His gaze flicks to Enoch who is still trying to charm credits out of the line of customers. "Will he allow you to eat if I bring it?"

I nod, not really knowing if it's true. No one has ever brought me food before.

I feel like I'm in a state of suspended animation while he's gone. I'm afraid to hope for him to return. Afraid to anticipate that he'll come back at all, much less bring food. My mouth didn't get the memo, though, because I'm salivating like Pavlov's dog. We've been on Fairea for months now and I've seen thousands of people walk by with *revensell*. God knows I'd love to taste it.

I'm only slightly surprised when he returns with the huge slab of meat in hand as well as lots of strips of soft cloth they use for napkins. My gaze flicks toward Enoch who catches my glance and makes a long assessment of Abraxx. I don't have to be a mind reader to know he's figuring out how much he can charge the male for a sampling of my charms. That's what the old bastard calls it—sampling my charms. Asshole.

Abraxx hands me the *revensell* and I dive into it, scarfing down the first few bites like a feral animal. A moment later, though, I say, "This tastes as amazing as it smells." Halfway through my sentence, I can feel a speck of meat on my cheek from devouring it like a wolf. I flick it off and attack the leg again.

"Good," he sounds indulgent. When I glance at him, the warm look in his eyes would never reveal he's watching a primitive female inhale her food like a starving animal.

"Sorry," I say, my mouth full of food. I just can't help myself.

"No apologies necessary. I know what it's like to be hungry."

I quit chewing even though there's a big chunk of meat in my mouth, then look at him. His tone was hollow, and his gaze is far away. Yes, I do believe this male knows exactly what it's like to be hungry.

"Want some?" I ask belatedly as I extend the partially ravaged hunk of *revensell.*

"No, thank you. My appetite's off lately," his voice is soft, like he's revealing a secret.

I like this male. It's not just that he fed me. He's kind. Maybe the fact that something is troubling him calls to the troubled part of me.

"What planet are you from?" he asks, his ice-blue gaze pierces into me as if he really wants to know. How sad that we get to start off with me telling him a great big lie.

Humans and Morganians can only be told apart by DNA testing. Slavers scoop us up for free from Earth and make one-hundred percent profit when they sell us. We may be outlawed, but it's an open secret all over the galaxy that human women are everywhere. Since humans are illegal, we're taught early in our servitude to tell outsiders we're from Morgana.

"Morgana."

His gaze flicks up and to his left. Does he know I'm lying? How, I wonder.

"That's interesting. I live with a group of human females. I could swear your speech sounds human."

"Humans are prohibited in space. Everyone knows that," my words are sharp, but the tone isn't. He knows other Earth women? Lives with them? I would love to know more.

"It's an open secret they're being abducted every day," he replies. "Perhaps you didn't know Fairea is a safe zone. Freed humans are allowed to stay on this planet unmolested. They don't even have to claim they're from Morgana." He looks straight into me as if he's trying to find my soul. Waiting for me to tell him the truth.

"Is that so?" I hedge.

"Fact. I looked it up on the Intergalactic Database. What do you think, Juno? If you were a human, would you want to stay on Fairea? Would you want to stay in a protected compound with others of your kind?"

Is he crazy? Why ask a question when you know the answer?

"I'm certain an Earth female would love to be in a safe place with others of her kind. If she wasn't a slave." My gaze flicks to Enoch again.

"I can't promise you anything, Juno. I'm not in charge. I know what it's like to get your hopes up and have them crushed. I don't want to do that to you—." He pauses as if he's having an internal debate. "Would you want me to try?"

"I'm a slave," I repeat. Nothing good happens to slaves.

"There's a price for everything," he says.

Suddenly, his words sound ominous. Yes, there certainly is a price for everything. I've discovered that time and again out here in space.

"And your price, *Numan*?" He's no longer Abraxx, the kind male who brought me food. He's going to demand a price. The hope that had been flickering in my chest, a feeling I haven't experienced in years, is dashed. Everybody has an angle, and this Numan has one too. At least it looks like he's going to be upfront about it.

His head tips back in dismay as his eyes flare. I surprised him.

"I want nothing from you," he sounds offended.

"What does that mean?" The words are out of my mouth before I can censor them. Is he buying me for his master? I can't see his neck, does he wear a slave collar too?

"I want nothing from you, Juno. I meant your owner will be able to name a price for you. No matter how much he values you, there's always a price. I understand your skepticism. I was a slave for fifteen *annums*.

"No one gave me anything. Well, no one gave me anything but shit and pain for a long time. Certainly no offers of freedom or sanctuary until three weeks ago when we were rescued and provided with a safe place to live. I can't prove I'm telling the truth, though, nor can I expect you to trust me."

The words 'out of the frying pan and into the fire' float through my brain when he stands straighter and starts fingering his wrist-comm as if he's just remembered he has one.

"Actually, I *can* prove I have something to offer. Wait." He pauses until he connects to someone via his wrist-comm. After exchanging greetings with a woman who speaks English, he says, "Dawn, tell my acquaintance Juno where we live."

My heart leaps in my chest. I haven't heard English except through my subdural translator in six years. Abraxx steps closer so we're hip to hip, then moves his hand across his body so I can see the vid on his wrist.

"Tell her about Sanctuary?" a woman asks in English. She's human. I have no doubt.

"Sanctuary?" I ask, the *revensell* hanging from my hand, temporarily forgotten.

"Yes."

Poor Dawn must have no idea what this call is about.

"Tell her why it's named that," Abraxx prompts.

"We're all free. We want to create a place where freed or escaped slaves can establish their lives in peace."

An electric rush flies through my body as her words reverberate in my head. A human woman is talking about sanctuary.

"You're on Fairea?" I ask.

She nods.

"You live in a safe place?" I ask.

"Uh yeah, but I don't know if you can come. We've never taken in a newcomer before. I don't know the protocol."

Just as quickly as that electricity flew through my body, it disappears. If it seems too good to be true, it probably is. That's what my dad used to say.

Abraxx steps aside and speaks quickly into his comm. After a long pause, he begins another conversation; this time I hear a male voice on the other end. I sidle over, not being subtle or even trying to hide the fact that I'm eavesdropping.

Abraxx is talking to not just a male but a different female who is also definitely human. It seems these two are both in charge, and not on the same page. Interestingly, it's the alien male who quickly agreed to rescue me, and the human female who is arguing against it.

"We're not in a position to spend our money on non-essentials," she says, "and *she* is a non-essential."

"Naomi, we all agreed to help human refugees," the male argues.

"Dhoom, I agreed to do that once we are well established here. If an Earth woman arrived at our gates unencumbered, we might be able to allow her to stay. Having to *buy* her? No. We've barely been here three weeks. We have supplies and livestock to purchase. It's too soon to start collecting a menagerie of additional mouths to feed."

I watch as my fate is discussed by two people who've never met me. Abraxx has said nothing until now.

"I'm going to negotiate a price," his voice is firm, "and then I'm going to ask you two for a loan. We agreed we would all split a percentage of the profits at the end of each *annum*. I'll return my share until she's paid for."

"We don't have the working capital—" the female says, but Abraxx terminates the comm in the middle of Naomi's speech.

I'm breathing fast, my heart pounding in my chest. There's a place of safety nearby where humans are free? I might not have to wear this slave collar for one more day? Is this a dream?

"You'll come with me if I do this?" he asks.

"What's the price?" I encountered little altruism on Earth, and certainly none since I was stolen from my bed in the middle of the night.

"None."

My mouth opens to say yes, but I stop myself before another word comes out. Didn't he just say there's a price for everything? He was right.

"The answer is no unless you give me a price. There's no such thing as free. You need to name a price and I'll decide if I want to pay it. If I say yes, you can expect me to keep to my word. And when it's paid, I owe you nothing. You understand? Nothing."

Chapter Two

Abraxx

Until now, I knew only a few things about this female. She's pretty, dances beautifully, and hasn't eaten in a long time. I just learned she's smart and strong-willed. I like her more now.

"I understand," I say, then pause. She wants a price. She needs one. It will give her a feeling of control over her destiny. I'll give her a price, but first I need to decide what it is.

I'm a free adult male for the first time in my life. No female has interested me in *annums*, but this one does. I feel like I'm getting one chance, and I want to take advantage of it.

I immediately know what I want. My cock does, too. But it takes me long moments to finish my internal debate as the line in front of Enoch dwindles. Although I had a lengthy argument with myself, there was never a doubt about what I'm going to propose. I wonder if she'll accept.

"I want you to dance for me for thirty days. Fifteen *minimas* a day. A private dance, just you and me."

She studies the tips of her shoes, her top teeth pulling at her bottom lip.

She thinks for long moments. Finally, her gaze flicks to Enoch and her mouth pinches tighter. When I glance at him, I see the line is gone and he's talking to his last customer. We only have a few moments before he'll interrupt our conversation.

"Just dancing?" she asks as her gaze pierces me. "Nothing more?"

"Nothing more," I reply.

After she nods at me, I turn on my heel, make sure my *sha'rill* covers everything but my eyes, and pace to Enoch.

The Thracian is tall, at least a hand's breadth taller than me, with coarse humanoid features mostly covered by a shaggy gray beard. Although Juno figured out how to stay clean while she lived with him in that little wagon, the same can't be said for her owner. My nose tells me neither his clothes nor his body have been washed in quite some time.

"What can I do for you, stranger?" his voice is oily. It's the voice he uses to persuade people to buy things they don't need and didn't even know they wanted until they saw his dancing female and heard his pitch.

"How much for the slave?" I pin him with my gaze and vow to myself not to glance her way until the negotiation is over. I don't want him to get a whiff of how interested I am.

"For the night? One thousand credits."

"I want to buy her from you forever," I gaze over his shoulder, trying to look uninterested.

"Fifty thousand credits," he says without hesitating.

I don't have to fake my shock. My head tips back in surprise and my eyes fly open. I'm glad my *sha'rill* covers my features; I want to enter this negotiation with at least a small edge.

"I want to buy one slave, not an entire dance troupe," I protest.

"Fifty." He spears me with his rheumy gaze. Now that I'm close, I can see the cloudy cataracts obstructing his vision.

"Two thousand," I counter. "She's human. Illegal." I give him a hard stare. I should save this bargaining chip for later, but I don't have the patience. Mentioning she's human should give him the impression I might report him to the authorities. Although humans aren't illegal here, perhaps he doesn't know that.

"Not here, brother. I don't plan on leaving Fairea. The Feds can't touch me here."

Drack.

"Five is as high as I can go," I offer as I wonder how many *annums* it will take me to earn five thousand credits. It suddenly strikes me how impulsive I am. I shouldn't have done this. What was I thinking?

"She brings in the crowds. I can't part with her."

"Everything has a price," I coax.

"Her price is fifty thousand. She'll be hard to replace."

A week ago, Naomi and Dhoom filled our comm bracelets with a small amount of credits for things like going to the fair or buying sundries. I have no idea what a credit will buy, other than the *revensell* which cost fifteen. I do know I'll probably die of old age before I can pay back fifty thousand credits.

"I'd like to go with him," Juno tells Enoch. She's stepped forward and places her hand on the small of my back. A jolt of lightning arcs through my body at just her soft touch. I have to use all my self-control to keep my tail from wrapping around her waist and tugging her closer.

"Fine." He shrugs as if he's acquiescing. "I know you have a secret stash of credits in that little bag where you keep your clothes. What's in there, slave, fifty credits? Add yours to his and I'm sure you can buy your freedom," he scoffs.

"Can we put our heads together?" she asks softly, her head cocked.

"Take all the time you need as long as it's less than two *minimas*." He turns his back and douses one of the torches illuminating the performance area.

Juno and I walk to the wagon where we spoke earlier.

"You're going to take me to the Sanctuary?" she fires the words at me swiftly, leaving no doubt in my mind that we do, indeed, have less than two *minimas*.

"Yes."

"I'll be safe there?"

"I vow it."

"Is there a medic there?"

"Yes?" She's hinting at something, but I have no idea what.

"Reach down and break my ankle. Do it now before I change my mind."

"What? No," I say emphatically. I'm shocked and horrified she would ask me to do this.

"A dancer with a broken ankle is of no use to him. He sells my body when he needs to, but tithes some of the money to his God afterward. He doesn't like to sell me unless he's desperate. If I can't dance, I'll be a burden. A mouth to feed with no way of earning her keep. Please, Abraxx, bend down, grab my leg and break my fucking ankle before I have time to regret this decision."

"You're serious?"

"As a heart attack."

I don't know what this means, but her face is sober, and she's nodding solemnly.

"Do it."

"It will hurt," I warn, trying to dissuade her.

"Like the devil, I know. Now, Abraxx. Please? You said you were a slave. What wouldn't you have done to gain your freedom?"

"Nothing," I answer. It's a swift response. How many times have I lain in one cell or another asking myself that question? I would have done anything to barter for my freedom, no matter the pain or the shame it would have caused. In my darkest times, I was willing to die to get my ultimate freedom. I don't want to die anymore. I'm free and I want to live. And so does Juno.

This realization breaks through my paralysis. Even though it goes against every fiber of my being to hurt a female, I can think of no other solution. I bend on one knee with my back to Enoch using my long *sha'rill* to hide what I'm about to do.

I lift her right foot and place it on my thigh. She braces her hands on my shoulders. Before I snap her ankle,

I pull down the folds on my *sha'rill* and expose my face and *brill* to her. She's trusting me to take care of her, the least I can do is let her see the face of the male who's going to break her bone.

I expect to see shock and disgust written on her exquisite features. Instead, her expression softens for the swiftest moment. "You have a kind face," she says, then gives me a pointed gaze and urges, "Do it."

After putting one hand on top of her foot near the ankle, I graze my other hand along the outer edge of her leg and grip her shin.

"On three," I tell her. "This will hurt. Sorry. One, two . . ." Before I get to three, I pull her foot sharply inward, and faster than she can blink, I snap her bone, praying it's a clean break.

She screams loud and sharp, then long and low. I stand and surround her waist with my arm, helping her bear some of her weight. It's the only show of comfort I can get away with in front of her owner.

Hearing Enoch hurry to us, I cover my face again.

"What have you done?" he bellows.

"I stepped on it wrong," she tries to cover for me, although our plot would be obvious to even the most simple-minded observer.

She's panting through her teeth in obvious pain. After reaching out to hold my forearm, she leans on me and moans again.

"She couldn't be worth much to you now," I say with false bravado as I belatedly wonder if I can be charged with willful destruction of property.

"Give me the five thousand, *motherdracker*," Enoch seethes, so angry his words flew out accompanied by spittle.

"She's not worth that much anymore. She can't dance; she can't even walk." I don't know why I'm trying to bargain him down when Juno is in so much pain. Her panting is quicker now, and she's clutching my wrist at her waist as if it's a lifeline.

Looking down, I can see the ankle turning purple, swelling as we speak. Her eyes are closed, jaw clenched and she's moaning in soft little grunts.

"Four," Enoch offers.

"Three and we're done," I say firmly.

As soon as he gives me a tight, angry nod, he stomps away to attend to a new customer. I keep my arm around Juno's slim waist as I comm Sanctuary.

"Dawn, transfer three thousand credits to my card."

"Oh shit!"

I can see the whites all around her irises.

"Naomi and Dhoom have been arguing since you hung up. I don't have the authority . . ."

I use my wrist-comm to show her Juno's face contorted in a grimace of pain. "Please, Dawn. If you were this human, hurt and still wearing a slave collar, what would you want someone to do?"

"Abraxx, that's not fair! Of course I want to help her, but . . ."

"Please," Juno grits through her pain. "I'll work to pay it back."

"I'm going to get into so much trouble. We all are," Dawn grumbles as she enters the transfer into her computer.

"I'll pay it back to them," I say. "And I'll make it up to you somehow. This female is human. She should be at Sanctuary."

As soon as the transfer is complete, I call Enoch over and hand him my card. While he runs my credits, I ask Juno if there's anything in the wagon I need to retrieve for her. Her face is pale. She stops moaning and opens her eyes. She's still panting and has a death grip on my arm, but there's a glimmer of hope shining in her eyes along with her unshed tears.

"The pack on my bedroll, the one on the right."

I lift her into my arms, sit her on the top step of the wagon, grab her things, lift her back into my arms again, snatch the card from her furious former owner, and jog to my hover.

After setting her in the passenger seat, I slide in and maneuver us into the air. I only learned how to drive one of these things three weeks ago. When we were all freed and decided to stay on this planet and make a go of it, every one of us learned how to fly. It was exciting having the power and autonomy to determine where I wanted to go. For the past two weeks I practiced around the compound property. This was my first excursion outside Sanctuary.

Realizing I have no idea how to drive one of these at any but the lowest speed, I swallow hard and crank it up. I don't want the badges coming after me if Enoch gets second thoughts. I fly in the opposite direction of Sanctuary for a few *minimas*, hoping to give any authorities the slip, even though little Juno is leaning against her door, moaning in agony.

"How far?" she bites out.

"An *hoara*. Let me comm ahead."

We're all being cross-trained on many jobs at the compound. It's clearly Dawn's night to operate the comms. When she answers, I tell her Juno has a broken leg. She doesn't ask questions, she just agrees to have Pherutan, our medic, standing by for our arrival.

"Tell her she'll be safe here, Abraxx. We'll fix her up and she'll be free," Dawn says, her voice kind.

Even through her pain, I see Juno's features relax. Hearing a female tell her in her own language she's going to be free and safe must feel like a miracle to her.

Glancing over, it's still shocking to see her foot canted at an odd angle. Guilt surges through me because I hurt this beautiful, vulnerable female.

"I'm sorry."

"Don't be. I asked for it."

She starts breathing through her teeth again to help control her pain.

"I won't be able to pay your price now." She shrugs. "I can't dance." She returns to the noisy breathing technique.

I know this.

"That's fine," I tell her, wanting to rush the words out before other, more wicked thoughts spill from my lips. My cock and the primitive part of my brain have been conspiring since the moment she asked me to break her ankle. They'd already cooked up a new payment before I snapped her bone.

"Nope, it's not fine," she says as she shakes her head. She sucks in a harsh breath as if she just had a spike of pain. "It's a cruel galaxy out there. I want clear boundaries. No surprises. You need to think of another payment. Because at some point, I want my debt paid and off the books. I don't want to owe you anything."

"What have you got to bargain with?" I press, knowing she has nothing but the meager supply of clothes in her pack, the fifty credits Enoch mentioned—and her body.

When she doesn't respond immediately, I take my eyes from the screens long enough to glance at her.

"We both know I have only one thing to bargain with, Numan."

Even though my cock is tightly bound in my loincloth and covered by my loose *sha'rill*, I'm certain she can see it tenting the material as I consider her obvious meaning.

The greedy part of my brain is screaming at me to make a proposition. Instead, I ask, "What do you suggest?"

"Okay. You want me to say it? I'll sleep with you."

Interesting, that was exactly what I was going to propose.

"For how many nights?" I press.

"One." By the way her gaze slides to mine it's abundantly clear she knows it was a low bid.

"Not enough." I'm looking out the window again.

"Two," she counters.

If she wasn't in so much pain, I think her shoulders would be hunched. She knows her offer is preposterous.

"If you want to haggle so slowly," I chide, "I'll start my offer at an *annum,* you'll counter with three days, and we'll be at Sanctuary by the time we come to a workable compromise."

"One month. That's my limit." Her jaw is tight and then she looks out the window to her right so I can't see anything but her back. Her voice sounded watery, like she's biting back tears.

"One *lunar* is fair," I tell her, then comm Dawn again. "We're ten *minimas* away. Is Pherutan already at the infirmary?"

She disconnects after informing us that our medic Pherutan is ready to set the leg. It's only now I hear Juno sob.

"I think it's a fair bargain," I tell her. "Or are you crying because of the pain?"

"I'm in pain, but I thought you might be a nice male, Numan. You're a fucker like all the rest."

"Did you really think one night was fair? I have no idea how long it will take me to work off the credits I used to pay for you. I think one *lunar* is equitable."

Juno

Fucker. All men are fuckers. I haven't met a good one since I was stolen from Earth. What did I expect? He eyed me up and down when I was dancing just like every male in the audience. What made me think he'd be better than all the rest?

I finally work up the nerve to look at him one more time. I don't even know what I saw in him. Six years of slavery has obviously affected my judgment. I can't believe I thought he was kind. The hope I was feeling earlier disappeared like a bubble in a glass of coke. One minute it was there, the next it's disappeared.

One month. What have I gotten myself into? Did I just jump out of the frying pan into the fire? A surge of bile rises into the back of my throat as anger, regret, and the throbbing pain in my ankle swirl inside me. I swallow down the urge to vomit.

"Once a day, Numan. There must be limits on expectations. Once a day, no more than twenty minutes. Those are the rules." Asshole. If I let him have his way, he'd probably keep me in bed all day and only let me up to go to the bathroom.

"You only need to sleep twenty *minimas* a day? All the other Earth females seem to sleep all night just like I do," he sounds genuinely confused.

"What are you talking about, Abraxx?" Shit. I should call him Numan. It seems to piss him off.

"I . . ." he stops abruptly, then clamps his mouth shut so hard I hear his teeth clack. Then he's laughing. He even has the audacity to reach over and pat my arm. "You offered to sleep with me. I thought you meant sleep. You meant . . ."

Did this male just fall off a turnip truck? He just drove a hard bargain to actually *sleep* with me? As in saw logs? Hit the hay? Catch some z's? If I wasn't ready to pass out from the pain, I'd laugh my ass off about now.

"So . . . our agreement is that I'm to sleep with you for thirty days? No sex?" My voice is high and tight as I say that last word. With this latest turn of events I feel like I'm in an alternate universe. The hope that died in my soul a moment ago has just been resurrected.

"Share a bed. Thirty days. If anything else happens, it will be . . . mutual," his voice is reassuring and warm.

I think I'll call him Abraxx from now on.

Yep. Alternate universe. I think this one will be infinitely better than the one I've been living in for the last six years.

Chapter Three

Abraxx

My parents taught me better than to force a female to have sex. All my *annums* among coarse males, gladiators and jailers alike, haven't erased those beliefs. It would have been despicable to bargain her freedom for the pleasures of the bed.

Pleasures. An interesting thought for a male who hasn't experienced pleasure since childhood. I've heard the sound of *dracking* all around me in the *ludus* barracks. I was never a premier fighter. I never earned a female. I had to take the other males' word that it felt good, better than a hand.

After a while in the dungeon, I tried to tamp down any hope of . . . well any hope for anything. I ceased longing for my freedom, to be returned to my home planet, or for a family of my own. But although I could control my daytime imaginings, I couldn't stop my nighttime dreams.

In the early days, I'd often wake up with a hard cock after I dreamed of a female at my side. At the end, when lack of food and water robbed me of enough blood to fill my cock, I still woke up with thoughts of a soft female sharing my bed. Even my attempts to obliterate those desires couldn't force the dreams from my head.

It's selfish of me, I know. I should let her join the females in the mansion, to live with the other humans. She should be able to get to know them, make friends, start fresh. But don't I deserve to be selfish? Can't I have something that brings me a shred of happiness?

She's the one who insisted. She said she wouldn't feel comfortable owing me anything. I gave her a fair bargain. Her freedom for thirty nights in my bed. I'll even wear my *sha'rill* so she doesn't have to look at me.

I land the hover near the infirmary. I'll dock it in the hangar later. After hurrying to her side, I gently lift her and lope to the building. Dawn is there, holding the door open for me. I know little about Dawn other than she's human. Since we took over this compound, I've kept to myself and tried to keep out of sight. I've been told often enough that my species is ugly, it's why I keep my face hidden unless I'm in my room.

Luckily, Juno passed out soon after our arrangement was forged. She must have been in a great deal of pain.

I stalk past Dawn into the treatment room where Pherutan is waiting. He sets the medbot into action as he uses his medpad to scan the break.

"Clean break," he says distractedly as he programs the medbot to set the fracture.

I glance around, trying not to remember the last time I was in medical care after a fight. The Whelpie male I'd fought had been slow and stupid, but he was almost twice my size and once he disarmed me, he threw me halfway across the arena. I had a dislocated shoulder and broken shin bone. It wasn't the pain of the injuries that brings back the bad memories, though, it was the punishment I received from my trainer.

He derided me for my performance as he put pressure on the fracture. He caused excruciating pain, yet I didn't cry out. If I had, I believe he would have increased his torture or perhaps killed me. He was the type of male who enjoyed inflicting pain, both mental and physical. I banish the brutal memory and focus on Juno.

I busy myself removing Juno's pain/kill collar. Although I don't want her to wake up with the abominable thing around her neck, I wish she could have watched. It's an exhilarating, freeing feeling to dispose of that detestable hunk of metal after *annums* of wearing it.

An *hoara* later, just as Pherutan is putting the fitted brace on Juno's leg, Dawn enters the room and announces, "Naomi was fit to be tied. You won't believe some of the stuff she said to Dhoom when they were arguing."

Pherutan and I have the good sense not to comment.

"I've got her room all set up," Dawn says. "Everyone is asleep, but they'll be there to greet her tomorrow."

"That won't be necessary," I tell her. "She'll be sleeping with me."

Dawn's mouth pops open and her eyes narrow as she glares at me.

"That's what this is about? You got the whole compound in an uproar, used the group's credits that were earmarked to buy more *anlaks*, all to buy a piece of ass? Fuck you, Abraxx. I'm calling Naomi and Dhoom. They won't allow it."

"It's the middle of the night, Dawn," I remind her. "You will let them sleep. If we wake Juno, she'll be in a lot of pain, so I'm not going to do that. If she could talk, she'd tell you she drove this bargain herself."

"I don't believe it." Dawn shakes her head. "And I definitely don't approve." Her nostrils flare as she lances me with an angry look.

I glance at Pherutan. The male and I were in cages not more than fifty *fiertos* from each other for *lunars* as we rotted underground. In the beginning, I talked to some of the males. Dhoom and I developed a friendship of sorts. By the end, we'd all turned feral or depressed or were too ill to find the energy to speak.

When I look to Pherutan for support, though, his gaze flies from mine. He's a smart male. I wouldn't agree with my course of action if I were him, either.

"Because I need to pay back the credits to Sanctuary, she didn't want me expecting payment from her at a later date. She set the price. She'll be sleeping in my room for the next thirty days."

"That's contemptible, Abraxx. I thought you were a nice male." Dawn's face is disapproving, her lips compressed. She can't even look me in the eye. "If it weren't three in the morning, I'd wake Naomi. She may not have wanted Juno here, but I don't believe she'd allow *this*."

"There's time to sort this out in the morning," Pherutan says calmly.

"Promise us you won't . . . touch her until after Naomi and Dhoom approve of this devil's bargain," Dawn demands.

"Of course." I could explain our deal in detail. I know what they're assuming now that Juno shared her presumptions. I don't want to tell everyone, though. That's Juno's decision. I don't understand these Earth females and I don't want to shame her.

"She's ready to leave?" I ask Pherutan.

"You can see I've put her right leg in a plas-brace from knee to heel. Here's a medgun set to administer more doses of painkiller and an anti-inflammatory. Give her one dose every eight *hoaras*." He spears me with a serious look.

"It's not my place to judge, but Abraxx, if I find out you hurt the girl, I won't hesitate to administer justice."

"I vow to keep her safe," I say, my gaze never veering from his face. "I won't harm her."

After he nods, I gather Juno in my arms, keeping her covered with the thin, white infirmary blanket, and leave to carry her to my room in the males' dormitory.

"Dawn," I call as an afterthought when I'm through the doorway, "can you come with us? She'll need someone to remove her clothes and put her in a nightshirt."

Once we arrive at my room, Dawn banishes me to the hallway as she changes Juno's clothes.

"We'll all hate you if you hurt her," Dawn tells me as she leaves my room, criticism written on her expression. "Where will you go if we banish you?"

I understand. She wants to protect Juno.

"I have no intention to inflict any harm on this female," I tell her as I close the door with finality.

Just like that, I'm alone with Juno. She's lying in bed, the covers pulled up under her chin. Dawn put her near the edge of the bed to be as far from me as possible.

I take a quick shower and cover myself with a loincloth and a clean *sha'rill* before I leave the refresher. Now standing at the foot of the bed, I realize my folly. This female has been enslaved and traumatized. I can only imagine the things she's been forced to do. She was willing to bargain with me for sex when she thought that was what I wanted. I doubt this was the first time her body was not her own.

After grabbing a wet washcloth, I return to the bed and clean her face. She had been dancing in the dirt, and she's covered with a thin film of reddish Fairean dust.

I pull the covers down to wash her hands. They're tiny. I can't help but notice our differences, her small tan hands in my large green ones. Closing my eyes, I struggle with the urge to draw the covers lower.

Lifting the covers off the foot of the bed, I use the washcloth on her foot. Pherutan cleaned her right foot when he was setting it. I breathe easier now that it's not cocked at an odd angle.

As I clean her other foot, a pang of guilt slices through me as I recall her yelp of pain when I snapped her bone. She's small and hurt and so vulnerable. I vow to my Gods to earn this female's trust and never harm her again.

My baser desires urge me to slide the covers up, to look at her firm calves and taut thighs and higher. *She's dirty, she'd want you to clean her so she could sleep easier*, the vulgar part of my mind wheedles.

I toss the washcloth into the refresher, hurry to my side of the bed, and lie down before I can act on those urges. I have no right to her, no permission to touch her. Besides, she'd hate me if I did.

Juno

Pain yanks me from deep sleep. It's sharp and hot, spearing up my leg like a fiery poker. Maybe it wasn't the pain; perhaps my moan woke me. I'm in a room. It's been a long time since I've slept anywhere but in that gypsy wagon with Enoch, or out under the stars when I could charm it out of him. He'd tie my wrist, threaten to use my pain/kill collar if I tried to run away, then let me sleep on my bedroll outside.

That was the most freedom I experienced since my abduction.

Now I'm told I'm free. The room is reminiscent of a dormitory. Maybe fourteen-foot square, with a closet and an adjoining bathroom. There's a large window, and light is peeking in around the window shade.

Gravity pulls me to my right. I know without looking that Abraxx is lying next to me, his weight dipping the mattress in that direction.

Turning my head, I inspect him. So alien. Abraxx has those thick hair thingies, and his tail is currently peeking out from the bedding wadded at his hips.

His face is humanoid, just an interesting shade of mottled bluish-green. He's handsome in profile, his nose is straight and just the right size for his face. He has a strong chin, high cheekbones, and triangular ears that reach into his hair things. My initial reaction still stands—he's attractive.

His eyes pop open and his gaze flies to me.

"You alright?" he asks, his brow lifting in question. His brows have no hair, the skin is textured there so their movement punctuates his expressions.

"My ankle is killing me," I admit. "Some asshole broke it."

My attempt at levity has the opposite effect. Instead of bringing a small smile to his face, his eyes flare as he looks pained.

"I'm sorry. I—"

"Abraxx, I asked you to do it. Don't apologize again. I'm at Sanctuary?"

"Yes. Everyone's concerned about you. Furious at me, actually. They think I'm going to harm you, take advantage of you. When I told them you were sleeping here with me . . ."

"I'll tell everyone it was my idea," I reassure him. Even though I'm in a new environment and know nothing about this place or the people who inhabit it, a feeling of calm washes over me. I'm free. My hand flies to my neck and for the first time in six years, it's unadorned by the piece of tech that ruled my life with fear.

"I took it off while Pherutan worked on your ankle. No more collar." His blue gaze touches mine, telling me he knows exactly how important those words are.

"Thank you." My fingers caress the naked skin on my throat, loving the feel of it.

He lifts a medgun from his bedside table and tips his head. "Want pain medication? Pherutan prefilled this and told me I could give you a dose every eight *hoaras*."

After I nod, he touches it to my bicep and administers the meds. Relief is almost immediate.

"You have to stay off your leg for a while. The plas-brace can be removed to bathe but should be worn even in bed to prevent re-injury. Pherutan said he'd like to see you later today. I thought you'd want to tour the compound so you can see where you'll be living. You can meet everyone at breakfast, then we'll explore together. I haven't taken a good look around yet, either."

'Meet everyone' sounds ominous. I hope the way Naomi and Dhoom argued about me coming here isn't an indication some of the people are going to resent me. I'd better figure out how to pull my weight. Maybe I'll get a small wage and be able to pay them back myself. It shouldn't be Abraxx's burden.

He comes to my side of the bed and lifts me. I'm wrapped in a blue muslin gown similar to the one he wore last night and like he is wearing now, minus the head wrap. I wonder what else he did to me while I was out of it from the pain and the meds.

"I asked Dawn to dress you in one of my clean *sha'rills*. I won't harm you, Juno. I'll keep you safe."

Safe. I haven't felt safe or protected in a long time. He could have undressed me, actually he could have done a lot more. I was totally out of it last night, but he called in another woman to put me in a nightgown.

A moment later, after he's carried me to the bathroom, turned on the shower, and left, I have time to reflect. What do I remember from a movie I watched as a kid? It was about some ancient guy who was ever in search of an honest man.

I've been in space long enough to believe there is no such thing. No honest males. No one who doesn't have an angle or an ax to grind or a dog in the fight or an ulterior motive. Except Abraxx has done nothing to hurt me. He brought me food, bought me with money he hasn't even earned yet, risked the wrath of his friends, and all he got for his troubles was my promise to sleep in his bed. I'd know if he had sex with me last night. That's not something you can hide. I don't think he touched me.

I think I like this guy.

I haven't had a shower in a long time. There was a bathhouse not far from our wagon, but you had to pay one credit for a shower. Enoch made me pay for my own, even though I earned no wage. I snuck in a few times when circumstances were perfect and someone left the door open. But usually I washed in the sink.

I wish I could stand more easily. If I could, I'd stay in this shower forever. As it is, it's a hurried affair. I may not be able to feel pain because of the shot Abraxx gave me, but I can feel the deep throbbing that tells me I've been on it too long.

After leaving the shower, I sit on the toilet and finger comb my hair. Since Abraxx has no hair, there isn't a comb or brush in sight. I have one in my pack. As I recall, he brought it with us last night.

Abraxx raps twice and says, "I asked Dawn to bring you some clothes. I didn't think you would want to wear the dress you were wearing last night. Open the door and I'll hand them to you."

When I open the door, he's standing in profile. His hand reaches in with the clothes and my pack as he carefully tries not to violate my privacy.

Don't trust him, my inner voice reminds me. *He's an alien. A male. They haven't been trustworthy in the past.*

When I'm dressed in clothes that are much nicer than the worn-out ones in my bag, I pull my hair into a ponytail from the supplies in my pack. Abraxx has me climb on his back and carries me piggyback to their dining hall.

"How big is Sanctuary?" I ask as I inventory everything I see as we walk from the dorm where we're housed to the dining hall.

"I don't know exactly, but it stretches from the bluffs on one side to the river on the other. We'll explore later today if you're up for it."

The dining room is empty except for Dawn who I met by comm last night. She's looking at him like she'd rather kill him than give him breakfast.

"I'm Dawn, nice to meet you in person. I was in the infirmary with you last night when *he* brought you in." Her eyes cut in Abraxx's direction. The way she said 'he' was full of as much contempt as you can cram into one syllable. "Did you sleep well? Are you alright?" Her gaze flits to Abraxx and then back to me.

He told me everyone was furious at him. That's not fair; I need to clear that up immediately. I'm going to assume he didn't tell them he broke my ankle, or they would be even more angry at him—even though I practically demanded it.

"After I broke my ankle dancing, I would have been useless to my owner. Abraxx convinced him to sell me to keep the jerk from using me to make money the only other way human women are used. Abraxx didn't take advantage of me; he saved me from a terrible fate. I have a few rules I live by. One is to never owe anyone anything. I drove the bargain to sleep with Abraxx. The operative word is sleep.

"I woke in a lot of pain, but Abraxx gave me a shot. I'm grateful to him and everyone here." Dawn's expression doesn't soften, she just flicks her eyes from him to me. She's unconvinced. "I repeat, he rescued me. He didn't take advantage of me."

Instead of easing her mind, my words seem to provoke her wrath. Her mouth tightens, then frowns.

"You can stay in the compound. I know you heard Naomi and Dhoom arguing, but they quit quarreling and went to bed. I assume it's decided. It's not right that you have to pay Abraxx a price at all. We have a room all prepared for you in the mansion. It's much nicer than the males' dorm where you stayed last night. Whatever he told you, you owe him *nothing*." That last word came out with vehemence and earned Abraxx another scowl.

Her words make me think. She's right. I'm here now. If she's telling the truth, I can stay and don't owe Abraxx a thing. In fact, that's what he asked for. He never wanted to make that bargain; that was on me.

"She's right," he says as if he can hear my thoughts. "You don't owe me anything, Juno. Why don't you stay in the mansion? Get to know the other Earth females. You can start a new life."

"I'll think about it." I should speak with him privately. I've never reneged on a deal in my life. I don't want to start now.

Chapter Four

Juno

The high whine and buzz of a laser shot pierce the silence. I first heard that noise on Hyperion shortly after I was auctioned. Once you've heard the sound, it's unmistakable. Every muscle in my body goes into immediate high alert.

I look out the windows into the courtyard to see what's going on, but can't see anything. Adrenaline courses through my body. I want to run, but my broken ankle will make that impossible.

Words drift in from outside. It's hard to make out what they're saying, but I hear the word 'arms' and . . . the word 'rustlers'? What the hell? Abraxx runs to the doorway to investigate the mayhem, then hurries back to Dawn and me.

"Invaders of some sort. They're on hoverbikes, shooting weapons. I'll help you two to safety, then return to fight." He lifts me onto his back, tells Dawn to follow him, and lopes through the dining room, past the kitchen, and out a back door.

On our desperate run toward the mansion, an ugly male with bumpy mud-brown skin skids toward us on a hoverbike, a rooster tail of dirt spraying behind him.

"Stop! Get the fuck down!" he yells in a language my subdural translator struggles with. "Get the fuck down!" If I didn't understand his words, I certainly understand the force of his tone. This guy is armed and crazed and there isn't one weapon between the three of us. My lips are trembling and sweat blooms under my armpits.

He lets his bike slide out from under him and is now running toward us, brandishing his laser pistol. Abraxx eases me to the ground, trying to be gentle while not wanting to anger the crazy amphibian guy who's not more than fifteen feet away.

"Just leave the females alone. I'll give you whatever you want." Abraxx says, his voice soothing. He bends his knees to appear shorter and less threatening and places his palms toward the marauder placatingly. "What do you want?"

"Credits. Synth. Females," the males' voice is a combination of gravel and knives.

"Females are better after synth," Abraxx nods. Is he going to hand us over to the crazy fuck? "Follow me. How did you know we have a synth lab here?"

Abraxx places a palm on my chest with the same motion you'd say "stay" to your dog. Then he motions the male toward the dining hall as if he doesn't have a care in the world. "Our chemist made a new batch. It's prime," he says, showing the enemy his back as if he trusts him completely.

"Hurry, asshole," the male says as he follows Abraxx, appearing to forget about Dawn and me.

So fast it's a blur, Abraxx turns on his heel, headbutts the brown guy, disarms him, and kills him in a flash of light.

I'm stunned. Paralyzed. That happened so fast my brain is still catching up with my eyes.

Abraxx runs to me, lifts me onto his back, says, "Hurry," to Dawn and we take off for the mansion again.

"You just killed that guy," I say into Abraxx's ear.

"Yes. Killed him. Saved you both."

"Oh my God." My thoughts are still frozen as he runs us through the front door of the largest structure in the compound. "Thanks," I say shakily. My teeth clack together each time Abraxx's swift steps hit the floor with a thud.

"That was amazing, big guy," Dawn says, her eyes huge in her face.

Abraxx takes the steps two at a time up two flights of stairs as Dawn tries to keep up.

"Which one is Daneur Khour's old room?" he asks, panting.

Dawn runs ahead of us down the hall, and we enter the only part of Sanctuary I've seen that is in disrepair. It's a huge bedroom that looks like it's been lasered to smithereens. There are remnants in every corner of small shards of wood and tufts of feathers from pillows that have been shot.

"Here," Abraxx says as he palms a metal plate in the wall. A three-foot-wide panel slides open revealing a separate room filled with boxes.

"Khour's panic room," Dawn says. "We kept it stocked, once we figured out how to open it, but I never dreamed we'd need to use it."

"Come in," Abraxx tells Dawn as he steps over the threshold and settles me into a chair. "As soon as I leave, press this." He motions to a plate on the wall. "Nothing can penetrate this room. You'll be safe. Don't come out until you see me on the monitor." He points to a vid screen on a huge wooden desk.

He grabs two laser rifles from a stash of weapons leaning against one wall, slings one over each shoulder, and hurries out while he yells, "Shut the door! Be safe! I'll be back."

"I'll be back? Think he saw The Terminator?" Dawn jokes.

"Does this happen so often you joke about it?" I'm so terrified my heart is thumping like a jackhammer.

"Nope. It's our first time. I believe it's called gallows humor. I've never been so close to dying. Abraxx saved our asses, you know. If he hadn't lured that asshole away from us with the promise of synth, Abraxx would be dead and we'd be getting raped to death right this very moment."

My palm flies to my chest as the truth of her words hits me. She's right. We were on that guy's menu. We're just lucky Abraxx convinced him females are better after drugs. Taking care of that guy didn't even make him break a sweat.

"I'm supposed to be resting my ankle. Are you going to close the door?" I look at it pointedly knowing my heart rate won't slow until it's locked in place.

"Nope. I'm going to grab us each a laser rifle from Khour's stash." She nods her head toward the wall of weapons to my left. "Then I'm going to help you hobble to the window and we're going to take potshots at whatever is out there attacking our sanctuary. Unless you want me to lock you in here alone while I hold down the fort?"

I've never held a gun before. Certainly never shot one. But I've been given a second chance at life, and I'm not letting a bunch of marauding dirtbags steal it from me. Dawn's ready to fight? So am I.

"I like your style, Dawn. This is my home now too. Show me how to shoot."

Two minutes later we're each kneeling in front of a window in the bedroom, laser rifles in our hands. Dawn put a pillow down for me to kneel on and another one under my shin to keep my foot from hitting the floor. I've been so deprived of any sort of kindness just that bit of thoughtfulness almost overwhelms me.

A second rifle is lying along the baseboard under the window in front of each of us, ready in case the first one jams. An extra fuel canister sits between our two windows. Dawn showed me the trigger and told me all I need to do is point and shoot.

"Fuckers," Dawn says as she scans the area through the scope of her rifle.

"I'm not familiar with the lay of the land. What am I seeing?"

"Welcome to Sanctuary. Three weeks ago, two ships of gladiators came here to kill Khour. Little bitch that he was, he let his minions fight while he ran to that panic room we were just in to eat bonbons and file his nails.

"Bayne, one of the gladiators from the *Fool's Errand*, was lying in wait and killed the motherfucker when he finally snuck out of his hidey-hole. The males from both ships liberated the imprisoned gladiators and us five humans. When the fight was over, we cleaned up most of the shrapnel and wood shards but didn't put any effort into a remodel. Not in this room, anyway. None of us wanted to step foot in here. Bad mojo, you know."

"Yet here we are."

"Yeah, here we are because Abraxx wanted to keep us safe. He's officially out of the doghouse. At least with me. At any rate, it's our compound as far as the eye can see." She pauses, her full attention looking down the sight on her barrel. She almost pulls the trigger, then whispers, "Out of range. Look at those fuckers! Assholes on hoverbikes are trying to rustle our *anlaks*!"

Anlaks must be the herd of cow-like animals I see toward the far end of the property. The hoverbike guys are trying to round them up like they're on an old-fashioned cattle drive—space-cowboy style.

"It sounds like Armageddon out there," I whisper as I watch the fiery bursts of laser rifles.

"It looks like the guy in the courtyard was a renegade on a private search for synth. The rest of the action is way out in what we call the lower forty but they're moving our way. These rifles are supposed to be accurate to five football fields. I'm going to test the theory."

She steadies her rifle, takes a breath, holds it, and squeezes the trigger. I was so busy watching her, I didn't see what she was aiming at, but I do see a fiery explosion signaling one of the hoverbikes just hit the dust.

"Nice one," I say. "That was better than TV."

"Yep. Score one for the good guys."

Since I've never before even held a gun, I don't waste ammunition. The bad guys are too far away. Dawn watches the action through her sight and occasionally squeezes off a round. It's usually accompanied by the words, "Got 'em" or "Fuck."

The action slows down and after a few minutes of sporadic gunfire, finally stops. A woman and a huge dog descend on the *anlak* corral and appear to be calming the livestock while moving them back to their pasture. I can hear the *anlaks'* anxious bellowing from here.

"That dog is Bayne. Well, in his canine form we call him WarDog. He's the one we have to thank for killing Khour."

A shifter? I thought those only existed in romance novels.

A few males have appropriated the hovers that aren't lying in smoldering columns of smoke, and are riding them back to the main courtyard. Other males are forcing the three remaining rustlers toward the courtyard at gunpoint.

I breathe a sigh of relief when I see Abraxx's *sha'rill*-covered form heading our way, a raider in tow. "Is he pulling that big Anthen by the ear?" I ask.

"You're familiar with that race?" Dawn asks. "How long have you been in space?"

"Six years."

"Sorry to hear it. I'm proud to be part of the effort that brought you here, even if Naomi is still madder than a wet hen."

"I didn't mean to get anyone in trouble," I say contritely even as I thank my lucky stars I'm here and don't have to spend one more night in that wagon with Enoch.

"I don't think Naomi's knickers will be in a twist after the shootout at the OK corral. I think this home invasion will now be at the top of her list of concerns." She somehow cracks open her laser rifle and polishes something inside it with a castoff pillowcase she rummaged from under the bed.

She's like Sarah Connor from Terminator 2: Judgment Day, ready for anything and good with a weapon. I feel like Sarah Connor from the original Terminator—a pathetic woman in shock and of no use to anyone. "You learned all that in the three weeks you've been free?"

"I'm a Georgia girl, born and bred. My daddy took me hunting before I was of legal age. I was locked in that dormitory over there," she points to the low-slung building I slept in with Abraxx last night, "when the two ships of gladiators liberated us. Since then, I've taken charge of my life in every way possible. That includes target practice and being able to break down this weapon, clean it, and put it back together."

"Without you, I wouldn't be here, Dawn. Thanks."

"Abraxx surprised me last night. I thought he was a good guy until the moment he insisted you sleep with him. I've got to ask, what was that about?"

After I explain why I insisted on paying him, that I didn't want him collecting on the debt at some point in the future, she nods and smiles. "You're a smart woman, and if you were telling the truth when you said he didn't touch you, then he's a peach of a guy. And yeah, his saving our asses from that crazed amphibian guy didn't hurt. Let me help you down to the courtyard."

I lean on her as we take the elevator, then I hobble to Abraxx as he hands off his rustler to a big horned male with golden dreads that seem to be waving in the air of their own volition.

Even though he was in the thick of a gunfight and I was supposedly locked up in a bulletproof safe room, Abraxx is more worried about me than himself.

"Are you alright?" he asks, bending to look straight into my face and make certain I'm fine. Using his palm, he swipes an errant lock of hair from my cheek.

Now that I'm safe, my adrenaline kicks into overdrive.

"This is just a delayed stress reaction," I say as I glance at my quaking hands.

"I would have been crazy with worry if I hadn't known you were protected in the safe room."

I have the good sense to look away and ask about the guy he dragged to the courtyard. There are only three rustlers who made it out alive. They're all different species and seem to be in their teens. Dhoom has pulled them aside and looks to be interrogating them. I wonder if he's going to call the local badges or let them go.

"We don't want to call attention to ourselves with local law enforcement," Abraxx explains. "The young male I escorted from the lower forty pissed his pants in fear when he saw what we were capable of. He said all the adult males are dead and there are only a few females back at their encampment. He swears they'll leave us alone and won't return."

"Do you believe him?" I ask, enjoying his strong arm encircling my waist.

"They were terrified. There are plenty of *anlak* ranches down the road in all directions. They'd be stupid to come back here."

When I release a sigh of relief, he asks if I want to go to my room in the mansion for a nap.

"You promised to show me the property. Now that I've fought for it, well almost, I'd like to see it." It's only when I see the look of shock in his eyes that I realize I just messed up—big time. His fists ball at his sides when I admit we never closed the door to the panic room.

He drags me against his chest so tightly I can't help but feel the swift thump of his heart through his thin *sha'rill*.

"I should be angry, Juno." He tucks his head next to mine and breathes in deeply. I think it's partly to calm himself and partly to inhale my scent. "Why would you risk your safety when I left you safely in the panic room?"

"I'm not a freeloader, Abraxx, and I'm not a guest. I want to pull my weight. I was ready to protect this place from intruders. It's *my* sanctuary now."

"I was just trying to keep you safe, Juno, but you're a grown female. It sounds like you and Dawn weren't in danger, but . . ." He shakes his head. "I'm just glad you're safe now."

Although my meds address the sharp pain of the break, I can still detect the dull throb deep in the bone. Between fighting the ache and the aftereffects of terror from the rustler invasion, I realize I'm tired and could use a nap.

"Abraxx, I don't think today's a good day to explore," I tell him.

"Of course. Let me take you to your room and get you comfortable. The females' rooms are larger and nicer than where you stayed last night."

It strikes me that not three feet from me is a fine male. He took Dawn's strong disapproval and my less than wholehearted embrace of our deal and is acting as if I've decided to move to the mansion. But I haven't. I don't want to welch on our deal. I don't know why, but he really wanted to sleep in the same bed with me. If last night was any indication, that's all he wants.

"Feed me and take me back to your room, Abraxx. A deal's a deal."

He hustles me into the dining hall, sits me on a chair in the kitchen, and I watch as he makes sandwiches and grabs bottles of water and packaged snacks. After tucking them into a bag, he hands them to me and hefts me onto his back.

I like this position and the way he's uber careful not to brush my right ankle. He spirits us back to his room in the men's dorm and settles me onto my half of the bed. Before I know it, we're sitting side by side, our backs against the headboard as we discuss what vid to watch.

"After what we've been through, perhaps nothing with laser gunfights," he suggests respectfully. I turn to him, wanting to tell him how much I appreciate that he always recommends and never commands. After six years of slavery, it's wonderful not to have anyone barking orders at me.

When I look at him, though, I'm struck by the fact that I'm in a cozy t-shirt and leggings, and he's shrouded in the clean *sha'rill* he put on when we returned to the room.

I reach out and touch the fabric at his cheek.

"Is there a rule that you have to wear this?" I ask.

"My *sha'rill*? No."

"Why do you cover your face?"

"I don't look like you. My differences tend to scare people. I thought if I kept myself covered it would make you more comfortable."

I reach out to loosen the thin muslin hooked behind his ear, then let the fabric fall to his shoulders, exposing his face. He's close enough I can feel his breath whisper across my cheek. Neither of us moves a muscle as I inspect him.

I saw him just before he snapped my ankle like it was a brittle branch, then again this morning in bed, but there's something about this moment. It's so raw and full of meaning especially after our near-death experience. Well, his near-death experience. It just now hits me that I could have lost him. It's as if allowing me to see him is a gift. It's intimate.

I want to kiss him. It's a surprising revelation, although it shouldn't be. I recall the electric attraction arcing between us last night when we were dancing. I'd never felt like that before and it surprised me. I couldn't see anything about him except the vague outlines of his body and those piercing, warm blue eyes.

I stare at his lips, then back to his eyes. He feels it. I know he does. His gaze doesn't leave my lips for long seconds. Instead of dipping his head and brushing my mouth with his, though, he clears his throat and scoots away.

"There are some interesting vids about the ice fish on planet Branff." He fiddles with his wrist-comm to switch channels.

"Perfect. I needed a nap." After tossing him a soft smile, I slide farther under the covers to lay my head on the pillow. I'm really tired and could use some sleep, so I scoot next to him and move his arm so I can lay my head on his pec.

He keeps his hand away from me as if I'm made of toxic waste. I allow this to go on for one minute max, then reach up, grab his hand, place it on my arm, then snuggle back to where I was.

The warmth of this strong gladiator's big hand on me is safe and reassuring. I fall asleep peacefully.

We laze the day away with me dozing then waking up long enough to watch endless pictures of big-mouthed sharp-toothed ice fish menacing creatures of the deep on planet Branff. I think videos of paint drying would be more exciting, so it's the perfect recipe for more napping.

When I'm not snoozing or allowing the boring vids to put me to sleep, I'm munching on the food and snacks Abraxx brought.

"You've been a good host," I say when it's close to bedtime. "I'll need another shot." My pain rode the edges of my awareness until a few minutes ago when it took center stage. I have no need to be a martyr.

He grabs the device and shoots me with the combination painkiller/anti-inflammatory the medic provided.

"I'll be happy to take you to your room now. It's dark. No more *anlak* rustlers or synth addicts will be shooting up the property tonight. You'll be safe. Certainly, you'll be more comfortable in the mansion with the Earth girls."

He's right. If I'm going to sleep in my room, now's the time to settle in. It's the last thing I want, though, and I'm not sure why. For the first eighteen years of my life, I was a kid. I made few big decisions, that's what parents were for. For the last six years, I was a slave. I had no free will at all.

Where I sleep tonight will be the first big decision of my life. I don't want to make it as a knee-jerk reaction. I want to make it consciously.

My gaze flicks to the vidscreen so Abraxx will think my attention has been captured by my sixth hour of ice fish. It gives me a minute to examine my thoughts. I definitely want to sleep right here tonight, of that I'm certain. But why?

When I don't feel his gaze on me anymore, I turn my attention to Abraxx. He's handsome. And kind. And there's this interesting attraction between us we both felt immediately even though we were under the scrutiny of every soul in that big crowd at the fair. I want to explore it.

Then another piece of the puzzle falls into place with thundering clarity. He's safe. I can explore this in the sanctuary of Sanctuary. That clinches my decision.

"I'd like to stay here with you, Abraxx," I tell him softly. He remains perfectly still, so still in fact that I wonder if he even heard me. I'm about to repeat my bold statement when his head swivels slowly toward me. Even though I know he heard me the first time I repeat, "I'd like to stay here with you."

That handsome face is so expressive. Perhaps that's why he keeps it covered all the time. The galaxy isn't a safe place, and it's definitely not the place where you'd want strangers to read your thoughts. At first, the planes and angles of his face show surprise, shock even, then it expresses pleasure. And then he grants me a gift, a small smile that grows wider by the second. Did I call him attractive before? Handsome? The smile makes him gorgeous.

"Just to sleep?" he asks, his gaze laser-focused on me.

I have to respect a male who wants to ensure he follows my boundaries.

"Just sleep, Abraxx." The next thought pops into my head with the force of a Category Five hurricane and simply will not leave my brain until it launches from my mouth. "Unless you want to dance for me."

Did I really propose that? So ballsy! I was the one who should be dancing for him tonight, after all. So blatant! So sexual! Well, if it's anything like last night it will be.

His gorgeous face shows every corresponding emotion from surprise to contemplation to unabashed lust. A zing of arousal arrows through my body in response. When he swivels away, sets his feet on the floor, and walks to the foot of the bed, my mouth drops open in wanton expectation. I know why I asked, perhaps I'll never know why he agreed.

He fiddles with his wrist-comm and the vidscreen dims then becomes a picture of a crackling fire. Music springs to life through the speakers. The music is nothing like Enoch's fiddle we danced to last night. It's unusual yet familiar.

After a few seconds, I place it, how could I not? My mother must have been the only person in Missouri who loved to listen to the Javanese Gamelan. I used to make fun of her for it, but there's nothing funny about the music now.

It's obviously not the Javanese Gamelan, but it's close. It must be his native music. It's an exotic combination of flutes and gongs and cymbals and the xylophone. It's intricate and ethereal. Because it's mostly percussion, the pounding beat allows Abraxx to move in a sinuous flow.

I watch him move in a two-foot square at first, as if he's self-conscious. I want to urge him on but decide against it. I simply observe until his stage expands. Soon he's whirling from the door to the wall of windows on the other side of the room. His *sha'rill* enhances his performance as it swirls and billows around him.

His expressive face has changed from tight control at the beginning to wild abandon now. This male was born to dance.

Take it off, my mind chants. *Take off that sha'rill. I want to see your muscles ripple in the glow of the electronic firelight.*

Perhaps he has ESP, or maybe it's what he wanted too because he grabs the blue muslin at his shoulder and begins to unwind it. He twirls and whirls as the music's pace quickens. It seems an eternity until his top half is exposed. He's tucked the fabric from his upper body into where it's bound at the waist. I can see his mottled green skin from the navel up in all its glory.

He's dancing so recklessly he's worked up a sweat that reflects from the reddish glow of the vidscreen. My mouth is dry from desire. My loins ache from wanting him. My channel pulses eagerly as I clench my fists to control myself from leaping out of bed to stroke his chest.

I smell his exertion. It's nothing like the stench of Enoch or the boys in high school gym class. It's spicy and rich and reminiscent of a rainy summer's day.

I've never felt this level of arousal in my life. Not on Earth, certainly not in outer space. But I want Abraxx. If he were to tear off his *sha'rill*, join me in bed, and remove my clothes, I would have no ability to say no. None.

But he doesn't do that. The exotic music slows, as one by one the instruments fade out until only the xylophone plays the lilting melody, a mere remnant of what it was minutes ago. It, too, dies out until it's just one slowly repeating note that gets quieter, accompanied by Abraxx's right foot stomping in perfect synchrony until they both cease at the same moment.

"Bravo," I say in a whisper of choked arousal, not knowing if he'll even hear me; he still seems mesmerized by the music and his performance.

He nods his head in acknowledgment, then he grips the fabric to hide himself again.

"Please don't, Abraxx." I catch his gaze. "I wish you didn't feel the need to hide. Especially after what you just shared with me. It was beautiful."

Abraxx

I haven't surprised myself in a long time. *Annums*. Decades. When I was first stolen from my planet, I shocked myself. I found it horrifying to discover I could capitulate so easily. I had been young and full of myself when I was taken. I thought I was strong and had the convictions of my faith. I never would have dreamed that one blast from the pain/kill collar would convince me to violate every tenet I held dear.

I fought, though. I earned many more punishments, but eventually I was the compliant slave they trained me to be, doing things I found abhorrent. I learned I wasn't the strong person I believed I was. That knowledge, my disillusionment with myself, hurt more than the slave collar's punishment.

It's been a long time, though, since I found parts of myself I hadn't known I possessed. But I just found one. That male who danced the *Ivlong* for Juno? I've never met him before.

The *Ivlong* is forbidden by my sect on Numa. I'd heard of it in whispers from the older males when I was in my teens. I don't know why I sought it out on the Intergalactic Database just now, but my fingers punched it in before I could stop them.

Now that I've heard it, I understand why it's whispered about, and why it's forbidden. It pulses along your veins and burrows into your brain and awakens carnal, lustful thoughts that should be reserved for mates.

I only removed the top of my *sha'rill* so it would provide more layers of cover down below. I didn't want the size of my erect cock to make her ask me to carry her to her room in the mansion. I'm greedy and selfish and want to keep her in my bed. I didn't wish to scare her.

One of the reasons Numans are stolen from our planet is the persistent rumor of our sexual prowess. We're known for the size of our masculine equipment and the way our tail adds to our partner's pleasure. My people try to play down the rumors, deny they're true because it spurs pirates to steal more of my race as bed-slaves. If Juno had seen my bulge, she would have seen proof that the tales are accurate.

"Want to sleep in the mansion?" I offer. Her answer will tell me how much my dance, and my body, frightened her.

"No."

I wish I was more skillful and could read her pretty human face better.

"I need to take a shower." I enter the refresher prepared to stay as long as it takes to ensure the painkiller has done its job and put her to sleep.

Chapter Five

Juno

It's been a quiet morning. Abraxx stayed in the bathroom for so long last night it made his meaning clear—he was waiting for me to go to sleep. I wonder if he embarrassed himself.

Now that he's piggybacking me to the dining hall, he seems more his old self. It was as if he couldn't wait to get out of his bedroom. Maybe he was right. If he'd come to bed last night after his erotic dance, I wouldn't have had the self-control to say no to him. By the heated look on his face when the music made its final pulsing beat, he wouldn't have either.

I meet a few people over a milky noodly breakfast concoction called *sumra*. Melodie, an Earth girl, and Thran, a huge bronze gladiator, sat down next to us. Even though they just met when they were freed from slavery a few weeks ago, these two seem like an item. I wonder if people are thinking the same thing about Abraxx and me.

After breakfast, Abraxx carries me into the empty kitchen, sets me on a counter, and proceeds to make us a picnic lunch.

"I don't know how long we'll be gone," he says as he makes sandwiches in an efficient one-man assembly line. "I'll grab a pack with more pain medication and blankets in case you get cold. We'll hover around the property and come back when you want. I'll bring laser rifles and pistols in case we see raiders, but Bayne and Dhoom are both already doing recon."

He stuffs the sandwiches and drinks and hunks of cheese into his pack, secures it over my shoulders, and lifts me onto his back. When I drape my arms around him and settle my cheek next to his, I notice he's covered his face again. I can't help but wonder what people have said to him that makes him so scrupulous about keeping his face covered.

When we arrive at the hoover, he eases me into the front seat, then checks to make sure there are loaded weapons in the back. A few minutes later, we take off. At first, he circles the main compound, pointing out the males' dorm, the mansion where the females are housed, the gladiator fighting arena and barracks, and the stables.

People take ownership here. They all seem to be busily erasing all traces of yesterday's laser fight.

"Perhaps you should take me back to your room. I'm useless, but I don't want them to accuse you of not pulling your weight."

"Dhoom comm'd me yesterday, told me to let you recover last night and show you around today. He wants you to feel safe and welcome here. Because of the rustlers it's too late to feel safe, but Dhoom wants you to feel welcome."

I reach impulsively to grab his hand and squeeze it. "You make me feel safe, Abraxx. I'll be great here. Between you and Dawn and Dhoom, I feel welcome." He squeezes back, then focuses his attention out the front screen.

The buildings are all beautiful. They're chestnut brown and rose-colored in an almost checkerboard pattern. You can see the painstaking work the artisans made to have the joints line up perfectly. It's slightly whimsical and very attractive.

"Are some of these buildings older than others?" I ask.

"We've only been here a few weeks and are still piecing things together. I think you're right, though. The well is at the center of things like this was a primitive town centuries ago. It appears the buildings closer to the well are the oldest. Except for the mansion where you'll be staying. Although it's far from the center of things, it began as a smaller, older structure. Khour renovated and upgraded it from the castle it was to the mansion it is.

"There are mountains far to the west, the river to the north, forest to the east, bluffs and caves to the south," Abraxx informs me.

I'm fascinated as he goes on to explain in more detail than Dawn provided that Daneur Khour, the head of the MarZan cartel owned this compound. I've heard of Khour, of course. Who hasn't? He was the most powerful male in the galaxy. I'm pretty sure he's the one who funded the ship that abducted and then sold me.

"So, Dawn told me he was killed by the gladiators that rescued all of you. Then you bought this place?" I look out the window as we slowly hover over open fields. The property looks huge.

"It's a long story. I was in an underground dungeon with seven other gladiators. We were being punished for not winning our matches. Beaten, starved, threatened with death." His eyes pinch in pain and he turns his head to look out his side window so I can't see his expression. I can see the muscle leaping near his jaw, although no words come out. There's more to the story, a lot more, but I won't press.

"All the Earth females were being held against their will in a dormitory on the property. Two vessels full of escaped slaves were on a mission to kill Khour. He'd been tracking them for over an *annum* and they were tired of being on the run. After killing him and all his henchmen they accidentally found us males and freed us. Freed the females, too.

"They forged the bill of sale for the compound and gave the property to us. We're just figuring out how to live here, how to pay the bills, how to care for the gardens and livestock. We found a hoard of Khour's art and are selling the statues and antiques to add to the start-up credits the gladiators gave us for working capital. You heard Naomi and Dhoom arguing. We're also figuring out how to get along.

"We wanted this to be a sanctuary for the downtrodden, especially Earth females who have so few safe places to go in the galaxy. No one thought we'd start taking in newcomers so quickly, though."

I don't say anything, just watch through the windshield as acre after acre comes into view. There's a meandering river far off to my right and rocky bluffs to my left. There are mountains up ahead, and when I turn in my seat, I see a forest far behind us.

"You really own all of this?" We've been hovering for long minutes and we haven't gotten to the property's edge.

"We. *We* own this. You're one of us now."

My mouth drops open. I haven't met Naomi yet and don't know her motives for rejecting me, but according to Abraxx, I'm part owner now? What an amazing turn of events to go from slave one day to landowner the next. My hand creeps to my neck, fondling the naked skin. It's still amazing not to feel the cold metal there that has chafed my neck for six long years.

When I drop my hand to my lap, he picks it up and gives it a gentle squeeze. "Still hard to believe?" he asks. "For me too. I was a slave for a long time. Daneur Khour and slavery in general broke us all. I think everyone in the compound has some healing to do and not just the physical kind."

We're approaching the craggy mountains. There are trees near the ground, but higher up the mountain the trees become sparse. It looks as if it would be a hard climb to reach the top.

"Can you fly us over the river?" I ask, fascinated by everything I see. I've been in space a long time. I've flown in hovers before, but there's something about being a free woman. About having even the tiniest amount of ownership of what my eyes are surveying. I try to let the feeling sink in.

The three Fairean suns are in an arc overhead, their light reflecting like diamonds off the water below.

"This is how I found the fair two nights ago," Abraxx says. "I followed the river, and it took me directly to it," his voice is deep and husky—masculine.

His shoulders are relaxed. It's good he can finally loosen up around me.

We explore the boonies for a while, but when we see throngs of people, I ask him to turn around.

"I have no desire to see the fair," I tell him. I was there with Enoch for months. I know every smell, every kind of lowlife, every scam, and every dirty look as if I'm lower than the gum on someone's shoe. I don't want to return.

Abraxx mentioned being a slave and touched on being held in a dungeon deep in the soil. You don't live through something like that without it fucking with your head. You don't escape trauma without being traumatized. I certainly haven't.

"I hear there are caves on the other side of the property. Want to explore?" he asks.

I was just in a dark place in my head, perhaps he was too. Keeping active sounds like a great idea.

"I don't know how much exploring I can do," I motion to my broken ankle, "but I'm game if you are. You'll have to carry me."

"Yes. I like carrying you."

I wish I could read his face, but it's covered. I think he was flirting with me.

"How about we make a deal? Let's have fun today. Let's do what we want. And . . . let me see your face."

His gaze darts to me, perhaps double-checking that I really want him to remove the fabric. He slowly releases the muslin from behind his ear, then pulls it off his head, allowing the voluminous material to fall to his shoulders.

He glances at me again, assessing my reaction.

"What do you call those?" I almost touch one of the ropes of flesh on his head, but don't want to violate his space.

"*Brill.*"

He gently grips my wrist and brings it to his head, silently giving me permission to touch. They're thick cords of flesh. The skin is warm and pliable. His lids shutter closed for a moment as his demeanor softens, then he appears all business as he glances out the window again.

"What are they for?" I ask as I surround one near the root and slide my hand to the tip.

"What is *your* hair for?" he asks.

He flashes me an attempt at a smile.

"Protection, I guess," I answer.

He reaches out, grasps a strand of my hair, and twirls it around his finger.

"And decoration," he adds, then looks out the front window.

He's sweet and tentative and definitely flirting. After consulting with myself for the briefest moment, I decide I want to flirt, too.

"And these," I say, touching one of his *brill* more confidently, "are pretty decorative, too."

"People of my tribe on Numa adorn them."

I inspect them more closely, wondering how I would jazz them up if I owned them.

"Bands of metal, piercings, adornments."

"Yet yours are plain."

"It's a rite of passage. It begins on the celebration of the eighteenth anniversary of one's natal day. Mine was celebrated being pummeled by my new comrades in a gladiator barracks." He said that without rancor, almost matter-of-factly. He carries emotion deep under the surface.

I press my palm to his cheek and allow myself to experience the attraction that's been swirling between us since the instant I first laid eyes on him. It reminds me of the sweet interest I used to feel about a boy in my class when I was just discovering the opposite sex. It's almost virginal, as if I could rewind my mind and start fresh with no memory of what I've endured over the last six years.

He turns toward me, his gaze flicking up and down and up again, and when his lips tip into a smile, it's a genuine one.

I haven't done anything spontaneous in six years. Prior to that, I was on a break between high school and college. I was partying my way through the summer with my friends before we scattered in four directions for higher education or full-time jobs. Having no homework, no pressure about doing well or getting into a good college was freeing. I don't think I'd ever been so unfettered.

It was utterly shocking to wake up on board a slave ship with a pain/kill collar around my neck. My world was transformed in an instant.

I'll never again be the Juno I was that day six years ago when I went to bed without a care in the world, but maybe I can create a new Juno who isn't afraid of being beaten and forced to do things against her will. I'll settle for that. Perhaps I can start that transformation today.

A few minutes later, Abraxx hovers to a stop in front of high stone bluffs.

"See that?" he points to a hole in the rocky face. "I believe we found a cave. They say there's a whole system of them under this part of the planet. Ready?"

"I'm game." Yes, I'm game, not just for exploring this cave, but for reinventing myself and starting a whole new life.

Chapter Six

Abraxx

When our gazes caught and connected at the fair the other night, I thought perhaps Juno's owner had given her drink or drugs to release her inhibitions so she could dance. When she agreed to come with me, I assumed it was just as she implied, that she would do whatever it took to escape slavery—even if it meant breaking her ankle and leaving the fair with a Numan.

But the way she looked at me as I danced last night, how she's looking at me now and her tender touch of my *brill*, this isn't just about the bargain for her freedom. I believe she's attracted to me.

After striding around the front of the hover, putting her on my back, and starting toward the cave, I return to grab a laser light and laser pistol from where they're stashed under the seat.

She eyes it warily. "I thought you said you didn't think the rustlers would return."

"When Khour wasn't murdering or torturing people, he was killing animals. He brought in herds of *crindles* to hunt. They're large, hairy, scuttling creatures that have an appetite for humanoids. Their population is growing fast because they have no natural predators.

"We supplement our income by killing them and collecting the bounties the government has offered to stop the exploding population of the deadly beasts."

"Large, hairy scuttling beasts. Great."

"I'll keep you safe." I may not have been the best gladiator in the galaxy, but I'm well trained in all the fighting arts, know how to use laser weapons, and I will protect the female.

As a boy on Numa, my village was near a cave system. I was always a solitary child, having no siblings, so it wasn't unusual for me to fill a pack with food and explore the nearby forest or caves all day.

With Juno on my back, though, I won't stay long. I'll just get a taste of what's inside.

Often, caves have wide mouths, but this one isn't much bigger than the doorway to my room back at Sanctuary. As soon as we enter, I'm struck by humid warmth, which is odd. Usually caves maintain a constant, slightly cool temperature.

The craggy walls are slate gray. My small laser light reveals a domed chamber maybe twice the size of my room at the dormitory.

"Here, point the way," I encourage as I hand the light to Juno.

She illuminates the walls and finds two corridors branching from the main entry hall. When she points the light to the one on the left, I stride through the opening and down the narrow passageway. Holding her legs against me with my forearms, I keep the laser pistol at the ready, taking my job as her protector very seriously.

"I love caves. We had one about an hour from where I grew up called Meramec Caverns. I seem to remember caves are always a steady fifty degrees. This is way warmer than that," she says.

"I don't know what fifty degrees means, but you're right, I've never been in a cave this warm."

We get to another fork in the system and this time Juno points to the right. We're only a few steps down this corridor when I realize why it's warm here. There's a steaming pool of water tucked against the far wall.

Juno

"Wow! Is that a hot springs?"

"It looks like it. Can I set you on the ground?"

He carefully eases me down, then kneels at the edge of the almost perfectly round steaming pool.

He's about to stick his hand in when I shout to stop him. "Wait! How do you know it's not some kind of bubbling acid?"

"Good point."

He tears a piece off the hem of his garment and dips one end of the rectangular piece into the water. When nothing happens, he pulls it out and squeezes it in his hand. He walks over to where he left me near the wall of the cave and offers the blue fabric to me.

I feel the warmth of it, then put it to my nose. It doesn't smell caustic. On the contrary, its scent is fresh. I touch the tip of my tongue to it and notice only a vaguely metallic taste. It reminds me of a hot spring my parents took me to that was supposed to have healing qualities.

"Think it's safe to get in?" I ask. After having to sneak into the bathhouse at the fairgrounds for a one-minute shower for the last I don't know how long, the idea of luxuriating in a hot tub excites me.

He pulls off his sandals, lifts his *sha'rill* to his thighs, and sits on the edge of the pool. "Let's see."

He soaks one foot for a while.

"You're brave," I tell him as the foreboding music from <u>Jaws</u> plays in my mind. The water could be filled with sharks or piranha or tiny flesh-eating microbes, but his green skin doesn't seem to be affected.

"I think we're safe if you want to get in. It's the perfect temperature," he offers.

I used to be fearless. There was a bridge near my house where a group of friends and I used to jump off into a lake after we'd had a few beers. I guess living an easy life and never having anything terrible happen to you will give you courage.

I'm not that brave young woman anymore, though. I've seen too many horrible things and experienced far too much pain to jump anywhere without having absolute certainty I will be safe.

When I don't answer him, Abraxx stands and approaches. Before I know it, he's retrieved me and I'm sitting on his lap at the water's edge. My hip is nestled next to his body, and my legs are safely propped on the rock in front of me.

Perhaps he feels the tension in my muscles, because he nudges my head to lean on his broad chest.

When was the last time anyone touched me so gently? Gave even a moment's thought to my comfort? I shake my head. I don't even want to think about that.

"I can take you back whenever you want. I imagine you're tired. Pain will do that, it steals your energy," he says. I'm sure a gladiator slave knows a lot about pain. "The warm water feels good, Juno."

I kick off the sandal Dawn gave me and turn in Abraxx's lap so we're both facing the same way, then dip my uninjured foot into the water. It's hot. About as hot as my friend Jasper's hot tub back home. It takes only a minute to get used to the heat and then it feels divine.

After reaching down and releasing the fastenings holding the clear brace around my right ankle and lower leg, I set it on the rock beside me, then ease my broken ankle into the water and lean into Abraxx's chest.

"I feel your heartbeat," I tell him before I realize how intimate this position is, how comfortable I feel allowing the thoughts in my head to fly out of my mouth. You don't need to have a genius IQ or an advanced degree to learn your slavemaster is not your friend. I haven't spoken my mind since I was abducted from my bed in Missouri. It feels good to relax my brain's constant censor and say whatever I want.

He dips his head and nuzzles his nose in my hair. It's possibly the least sexual touch a male can give a female, but the way his warm breath ruffles my hair and the respectful way his hands hug my waist makes me wonder if sex with him could feel this sensual—and safe.

Our natural hot tub takes up about three-quarters of the room. The enclosed space feels secure and the laser pistol sitting on the rock floor only inches to our right ensures our safety. It's quiet here, peaceful. The humidity causes moisture to accumulate on the ceiling and then drip rhythmically into the pool below.

I want him to hug me tighter, so I put one of my hands on each of his and move them from where they're perched on my sides until his arms encircle my waist completely. I gasp and practically jump out of his lap when something grips my left ankle. When my shocked gaze flies to it, I see his green tail has gently wrapped around it, the tip drawing lazy circles on my calf.

"You scared me," I half-heartedly slap his thigh.

"Sorry." His body had become relaxed, his head on mine, but my gentle scold has him sitting straight as a tin soldier. I wish I hadn't done that.

"Think it's safe to go in?" I ask.

"Yes."

"You go first, I'll join you if the piranha don't eat you."

"Piranha?"

"Flesh-eating fish."

"Seriously? You have those on your planet?"

"Yep."

He lifts me and sets me at the water's edge, then stands, turns his back to me, and pulls off his *sha'rill*. I can't tear my eyes from him as he folds the cloth and sets it out of the way. A part of my mind, a very quiet, non-assertive part of my mind, clears her throat and mentions that staring is impolite. The other part of me grabs a megaphone and some binoculars and orders me to drink in the sight of him.

My first owner was a reptilian bastard whose face gave me the skeeves for the entire two years he owned me. My second owner was a birdlike fellow with a barrel chest, yellow feathers, and a penchant for backhanding me even when I was trying to please him. Enoch looked like a geriatric Neanderthal on his best day and Sasquatch on his worst.

Abraxx is beautiful.

His skin is mottled green with blue tinges. It's marred by the type of scarring you'd expect on a gladiator. If anything, it just makes him sexier. Did I say sexy? Yeah, he has the body of the statue of David. No. David's muscles look like they're for show. Abraxx's muscles look like he knows how to use them.

The loincloth barely covers his ass, but every other muscle in his legs and back is on display. As dim as it is in here even with the laser light illuminating the small space, I can enjoy the sight of his muscles as they ripple under his skin while he folds his clothes and sets them on the rocky floor.

And that tail, it's flicking in a not-quite-feline way. Maybe it's best described as slashing. It's sinewy and supremely sexy. He waits an extra moment to turn toward me before he steps into the pool. Is he shy? He'd have to be blind and half-dead not to know I'm perving on him. How could he not feel my appreciative gaze?

"Your body is amazing Abraxx." I had to say it. How could I keep that thought to myself?

Perhaps this emboldens him, because he turns toward me so gradually you'd think the world had decelerated into slow motion.

Interesting thing about loincloths. I hadn't realized before, but although they're designed to contain a man's genitals, they hide nothing. Nothing. In fact, they accentuate them. At least that's what Abraxx's loincloth does. It clutches his cock and balls in a way that would capture the attention of any woman from eighteen to eighty.

I try for a second, maybe two, to hide my interest, then give up on that entirely.

"Your face is amazing too," I husk through dry lips.

His skin is green, so I can't say he's blushing. He's embarrassed, though. His head dips slightly and his gaze casts down. He's self-conscious. I guess I should have expected that; the guy walks around among his friends shrouded in that *sha'rill* from the top of his head to the tips of his toes.

He sits on the edge of the pool as far from me as possible and slides in quickly. I assume he's more afraid of my appreciative stare than the possibility of flesh-eating fish.

"How is it?" I ask, hoping to lighten the mood.

He's standing with the surface of the water between his waist and his nipples.

"I don't think we're the first people to discover this," he says as he walks the perimeter of the twelve-foot in diameter pool. "The bottom is almost perfectly flat, and there are . . ." He pauses for a moment as he fishes his hands under the surface. "There are ledges here to sit on."

"I guess it makes sense that previous inhabitants of the compound did some chiseling to make the hot tub comfy."

"Hot tub. That's a good name for it," he says, nodding. Perhaps my intrusive ogling is forgotten.

He approaches me with his arms out like a dad waiting to pick up his kid under their armpits.

"My clothes," I say as I shrug.

"Take them . . ." his mouth is so dry he swallows with difficulty. "Take them off."

Abraxx may be blushing and stammering and shy, but he's not immune to what he obviously considers my charms. I stand, turn my back, and pull off the t-shirt and leggings Dawn provided. I look down at the pitiful bra and panties I've been wearing and repairing and patching for so long I don't believe any of the original fabric is still in existence, then turn back to him.

Did I think I was perving on him a moment ago? I stand corrected. What he's doing to me? *This* is perving.

The male can't take his eyes off me. They do a slow scan from tattered bra to threadbare panties, then slide north and south again. I have to clear my throat more than once before he shakes his head and returns to full awareness.

I reach out and grab him by the shoulders as he pulls me into the pool. Rather than just dropping me on my feet, he wades to the far side and sets me down as if I'm breakable.

Damned if he wasn't right, there is a smooth ledge under here. He slides next to me and sits with his hip nestled next to mine. Our backs are to the stone wall behind us so we have a good view of the room. Nothing is going to attack us here, especially now that Abraxx gets up, grabs our pack and the gun, and sets it on the small ledge behind us.

From the pack, he pulls out the sandwiches he made and offers one to me along with a bottle of water. I suddenly realize I'm starving. We eat and drink in companionable silence soaking up the peace while soaking in the hot water.

He asks about my leg, which feels great. Maybe the warm water is working its magic.

Here we are in the steamy hot tub. Alone. There's nothing to interrupt us. He's interested in me. That little factoid has not escaped my notice. Through the murky water, I can see his loincloth is definitely packed fuller than it was a few minutes earlier.

If he was merchandise that was branded as 'small, medium or large,' his package would be labeled 'wowza'. Or perhaps 'oh-my-God' size.

My heart is hammering in my chest, my mouth is dry, and energy is swirling in my pelvis. I can't remember the last time I felt desire—except for the last two nights.

Actually, I've felt desire for many things over the last six years. Desire for every one of my previous owners to drop dead. Desire for someone to kill them for one of the plethora of reasons they deserved to die. Desire to be back in my bed on Earth and wake up to have a do-over. Desire for freedom. Yes, I've had many desires since my abduction, just no desire for a male.

Until Abraxx.

Right this moment, the feeling of lust hurtles at me with the speed of a Formula 1 racecar. With a vengeance.

The part of me that carries the megaphone and never lets me get away with lying to myself, asks what is so wrong with wanting Abraxx?

Nice Abraxx? I reply. *The male who apologized a dozen times for breaking my ankle after I demanded it. The male who got himself in hock to the likes of Naomi for the rest of his natural-born life so he could buy me and then set me free. The male who refused my offer of sex because he's sweet and in this shithole of a galaxy has somehow found a way to retain some semblance of a moral compass. The male who practically slept in the bathroom last night rather than return to the bedroom and act on the electric attraction arcing between us? Nothing.* Nothing *is wrong with Abraxx.*

I turn to him and try to look him in the eyes but he's having none of it. He's studiously avoiding me and inspecting the rippling water.

"Did you have a girl back home on Numa?" I ask, wanting to get to the heart of the matter.

"No."

He's pretending he's fascinated with the stalactites above our heads. I'll just pretend we're having a normal conversation and answer the question he's too shy to ask me.

"I didn't have anyone either. I was taken at an odd time in my life. I was in between trajectories. I'd just completed one type of school and was about to head off to another. In the meantime, I was carefree."

"Carefree. That's a nice Earther word," he says, his voice deep and hushed as if he's confiding his secrets. "I guess I was carefree too. I grew up in a loving home and was learning the family business. My father was in charge. All I needed to do was show up each day and work hard. I was young and ungrateful and at times I resented it." He laughs ruefully. "I'd give anything to have it back now, though."

We both fall silent. I'm imagining what his life might have been like, and how in the blink of an eye he wound up as a slave, training to be a gladiator.

"We're free now," I remind us both. I pause a moment as I ponder if I should say this next part, then forge ahead. "I've paid a price for the last six years. I imagine you have too. I deserve happiness."

"You do. I'm certain you do," he says without hesitation, looking me in the eyes.

"And you, Abraxx? Do you deserve happiness?"

His gaze snaps from mine as he ponders.

"I've killed males," he says, his voice so low I had to strain to hear it.

I grab the hand that's sitting on his thigh. "Do your people have war?" I ask, getting ready to make a connection between being forced to kill someone in the arena versus being forced to kill someone in battle.

"No."

My head whips to him and I scan his face as I try to absorb this fact. Human history is so riddled with war, I read once that there hasn't been one day in recorded history where one human faction wasn't warring with another. No war? On another day I'll have to ponder what it would be like to live on a planet where people live in peace.

Although my attention had been captured by the steamy, swirling water, my head swivels so I can watch him when he answers my next question.

"Do you worry your God will punish you for what you did in the arena?" I detect a dozen emotions passing over his features one by one.

"I punish myself enough," his voice is a serious whisper.

His piercing blue-eyed gaze doesn't shy from mine. Inside his handsome head lives a tortured soul.

"We do what we have to do to survive. It's the first rule of slavery," I tell him earnestly. Goodness knows I've told it to myself often enough. I have a list a mile long of things I've done because of the threat of the shock collar. I'm not proud of them.

"I suppose."

"And what you did yesterday, Abraxx? Saving my life, and Dawn's. I hope you don't feel bad about that. It's the most heroic thing anyone's ever done for me. You could have run off and let him have us. I don't know anything about your God, but I can't imagine he'd disapprove of what you did to save us."

A look passes between us. Volumes are spoken without a word being said. I think what I just said helped him begin to make peace with himself. Even so, between the two of us, there's still a lot of pain in this room. With all the torment and shame and guilt, there's plenty to go around. I've suffered more than my fair share; I want to move beyond it. I want a circuit interrupt.

"When you were holding me a moment ago, it felt better than anything I've experienced in the last six years." The quiet intimacy has me sharing private thoughts with a male I just met.

"Aye."

His words may have decreased to monosyllables, but his facial expression is speaking loudly.

"Would it be so terrible if we gave each other comfort Abraxx? We've both been forced to do things that make us feel dirty. I wonder if there are things we can do together to make us feel clean."

It would be the first time I make a conscious and consensual decision about who can enter my body. I'd like it to be the kind and gentle male sitting next to me.

"I would like very much to provide you comfort, Juno."

He leans so close I can feel his breath whisper across my cheek. My lids flutter closed as I await his kiss, but I feel him pull away. Instead of feeling his lips on mine, his knuckles slide down my face from cheekbone to chin. The touch is soft as silk. It's so tender it makes me want to cry.

I've been alone and ill-used for so long. Maybe a moment ago when I made my bold proposition I was still on the fence, but after that one stroke of his flesh on mine, I know it's the right decision.

He brushes his thumb across my lips and I open my eyes in time to see him swivel toward me, tipping his head to watch me with rapt fascination. When a picture flits through my mind of other encounters—forced, swift, harsh—I push them away.

I'm here with Abraxx. He's touching me with tenderness. Lean into the feeling.

Dipping his head to place his mouth next to my ear, he asks, "Do you desire more than comfort Juno? Do you wish for pleasure?"

Pleasure? A burst of emotion flashes through my body. Dare I hope for that?

I nod.

"I've never been allowed a female. Teach me how to give you pleasure, pretty Juno. You give me the gift of your body and I will give you the gift of as much pleasure as I can bestow."

My pulse quickens. Maybe it's his heartfelt desire to please me, maybe it's the incandescent look in his blue eyes. It doesn't matter.

I'd thought my sexual response cycle had been irreparably broken during my years as a slave. By the squeezing deep in my belly and the pulse pounding in my clit, I realize my body isn't broken after all.

He begins with a kiss. The softest brush of his lips on mine. I take one last moment of conscious thought to order my mind to think of nothing other than what's happening right now. I hang a big 'Do Not Disturb' sign on my memory closet, then dive into this moment.

I don't want to miss a minute of his sweet kisses, so I immerse myself in the feel of his flesh on mine. The sound of his breathing mixed with the steady drip of the cold water slowly drizzling from the ceiling into the hot pool.

He nuzzles my cheek with his, then returns to my mouth to slide his wet tongue along the seam of my lips. I reward him by saying his name, then opening to him. His slick tongue enters me, tasting me as he moans from deep in his throat.

He pulls away far enough to tell me, "You taste so good, Juno." Then his tongue is back inside my mouth, exploring, claiming.

My fingers curl around his shoulders. They're hard and tight. He said he'd been starved for a while. I can feel bones that are too close to the surface.

The sound of our labored breathing and our lips smacking wetly against each other reverberates throughout the stone walls of the protected chamber. Missouri is hot and humid. On summer days the warm air smells fecund, fertile. That's what Abraxx smells like. It's not so much a smell as the promise of more. And his taste has the same potent heat.

The dim recesses of my mind notice my ankle isn't killing me as I straddle his lap. The stone ledge I'm perched on bites into the skin of my knees, but I force that thought out of my mind and choose to focus on the slick slide of my flesh as I glide down his body. My nipples, even through my tattered bra, are like chiseled points of granite as they drag across his naked green chest.

He sucks in a breath, then tucks me closer, his hands on the globes of my ass. His cock is harder than the stone we're sitting on. The level of his arousal shocks through me as I gasp in surprised pleasure.

After lodging my palms on the back of his neck, I curl them each around one of his *brill*. They're supple and sturdy, but what grabs my attention is the way his body stiffens as he sucks in an aroused breath.

This confirms my suspicion they're erogenous. My fingers explore from base to tip. I experiment with pressure and placement, and within a minute I've discovered he likes firm pressure at the spot where each *brill* attaches to the head. But flicking the tips makes him throw his head back and suck in a shocked breath.

"Like this?" I ask, plucking the tip the way I like my nipples played with.

His answer is to stare at me in surprise and wordlessly nod his head. The look on his face is the sexiest thing I've ever seen.

Emboldened, I grab the longest *brill* and suck the end into my mouth.

"Juno!" he scolds with a husky tone that sounds like he wants me to stop but means the opposite.

I flick it with my tongue until he shakes his head and says, "Too much."

I make a mental note to explore this later. Knowing he'll never figure out how to release it, I reach behind me to undo the clasp of my makeshift bra, then toss it to the side of the pool.

The appreciative sound of his grunt amps up my passion. His ice-blue eyes glaze over in lust. It's a potent sight.

Kneeling up, I position one nipple in front of his mouth. He quickly accepts my silent invitation and licks the hardened tan tip, flicking it with his tongue. Hissing between my teeth, I throw my head back in excitement.

That was a good appetizer, but I want more.

"Suck them. Nip them," I coax as I thrust my chest out to him.

He responds with sucking, nipping, then more flicking. I didn't even realize I was riding his cock—hard—until he tucks me against him even tighter.

"Abraxx," I hiss, splaying my hands across his back, learning every muscle and tendon by heart like a blind person reading braille.

His mouth is at one breast, one hand is at the other. He's plucking and nipping while his other hand palms one of my ass cheeks, helping me garner more friction as I ride his hard cock. His other hand grips my hair and pulls it so my chest is arched toward him, the column of my neck exposed.

It's only when I glance up that I realize it's not a third hand yanking my hair. His tail has entered the fray.

"Tail," I say. Not knowing how else to acknowledge how much I enjoy all the pleasures he's brought to the party.

He tugs my hair again, then his tail gently wipes a loose strand of hair off my forehead.

I'm panting and riding him, my head thrown back. He grunts in surprised pleasure when I grip his *brill* again.

He's torched my need, and I'm burning for him. Moving away just enough to put space between us, we remove our remaining clothes and throw them to join my bra on the stone floor. I straddle him again.

I'm so slick I glide along his cock with ease. My eyes are shuttered and now is not the time to perform an inspection, but he's different down there. He's got ridges that tantalize me on every arousing slide up and every exciting drive down. I've coated him with my cream even though the water's trying to wash us clean.

Pressing my lips to his ear, I whisper, "Take me," into his pointed, green ear.

He grabs one of my hands from his shoulder then presses it low on his belly.

"Touch me, Juno. You're so small. I'm too big for you."

Sliding my hand down his flesh, I grab him at the root. He was right. Definitely big. My fingers can't reach around him. Exploring upward, I'm shocked when I encounter a thick bulb. If the root itself was daunting, this new turn of events is foreboding.

My gaze flies to his. He's watching me through lust-filled slitted lids. When my hand travels higher, I find three ridges, then a thick, blunt head. While I won't be able to accommodate that bulb, I can get the top of his shaft and those three sexy ridges inside me.

"Teach me how to pleasure you in other ways, Juno. There must be other things I can do to satisfy you." His expression is so sincere. He wants to make me feel good even above his own pleasure.

"We can do this, Abraxx." I nip his collar bone, which elicits a sharp intake of breath. This is his first time. My slightest touch lights him on fire. It's sexy.

My knees still on the stone ledge, I tilt my hips at a better angle and use his ridges to heighten my arousal. I'm panting, my head tipped back, my nipples thrust near his face, and my slick nether lips are riding him hard. I bring myself to the point where I'm close to coming. If there will ever be a moment where he can fit inside me, this is it.

Grabbing him low on his cock, I fit him at my entrance and take his head inside me as I moan a sound full of both relief and need.

I startle for a moment when his hands go to my hips. Is he going to use them as leverage to jam me down on him? I'm not ready.

But his touch is gentle, steadying, willing to help but not force. I lean forward to kiss him. Our connection is sublime. There isn't an inch between our wet bodies. I'm plastered to him, feeling his body heat.

My core has relaxed around him, and I begin to move. Little movements up and down that thrust him deeper inside me with every downstroke. I thought I was in heaven until I hit the first fleshy ridge. No, *this*, this is heaven.

In just a few more movements I'm down to the bulb. I don't know about him, but I'm happy with this. When I glance at him, a bolt of lust sizzles through me. Look at that face. His lids are closed and he's panting through parted lips. I don't think I'll be hearing any complaints from him.

I slide all the way up, then down again. The ridges massage my inner walls in all the best ways. The bulb impacts my clit on every down thrust, adding more sensations to the mix.

"Fuck me, Abraxx," my voice is deep and low and hardly sounds like me.

"Don't want to hurt you."

"You won't. Just don't force me any lower than this." I hit bottom, my clit grinding against his fleshy bulb.

Bracing his palms against my back, he presses me close, then kisses me tenderly once, twice, three times. Anchoring me with his tail around my waist, he pumps into me from below.

His breathing is ragged, then devolves into grunts as he presses into me hard enough to give me just the right pressure against my clit, but not so hard that the bulb enters me.

Heaven. This is bliss. My water-slicked nipples are bouncing against his chest with every thrust. His breath is hot upon my face, and when I peek at him his expression could be in the dictionary next to the word 'ecstasy'.

It's the look on his face, a combination of arousal and surprise, that pushes me over the edge until I spasm around him. My inner walls gripping him, being tantalized and massaged by his ridges.

A deep, low moan is pulled from me as my orgasm ramps even higher, taking me to another level of excitement. My orgasm triggers his and he hugs me tighter as he jets into me. I feel his warmth bathe me as his release is accompanied by a loud bark of pleasure. Then another.

I collapse onto him, my forehead on his shoulder, every muscle sagging onto him.

When I regain my senses, I surround him in a hug and kiss his cheek.

"Abraxx," I say as I cup his other cheek with my palm. I want to say other things—tender things, sweet words—but clamp my lips together. I've known him two days. It would be ridiculous to pretend anything more than good sex happened here. Well, great sex.

Abraxx

I kiss the top of her head while my hand roams her back. What an extraordinary experience. What an extraordinary female. What a gift.

Numan males from good families do not have sex until they are mated. After my abduction, my owners withheld females from all but the premier fighters. Is this what the males bragged about in the *ludus*? They talked about the physical pleasure, said it was better than their hand, but they never talked about the emotional intimacy. Sharing this with Juno makes me want to know everything about her.

"How's your ankle? How's your . . . Did I hurt you?"

"You didn't hurt me, Abraxx. It felt wonderful. Amazing." She grants me one of her penetrating gazes. It's luminous and full of appreciation. I made her feel good. This pleases me.

"Juno, that was beyond anything I've ever imagined. I feel better than I have in fifteen *annums*."

She smiles and hugs me tighter. I kiss her, then lift her off my lap and place her on the underwater ledge. Lifting her leg carefully, I pull it above the surface to look at it.

"The swelling's gone down," I tell her, surprised that the bruising has faded.

She leans forward to inspect it, then glances at me quizzically. "That's odd. I bruise easily, and they stay a long time. Weeks."

As she rotates her ankle, I place my fingers gently above the bump on the outside of her leg. Her eyes widen in surprise. I don't feel any crack or separation or grinding.

"The pain's gone."

"It was hurting when you got into the water?" I ask.

"Yep."

"And no pain now?"

"Yeah." She laughs. "It was either your magical healing cock or the water."

"I'd like to think it was my cock," I say with a smile and a wink. I don't believe I've ever winked at anyone in my life.

"Definitely the cock. I guess you could bottle it and get rich."

"Do you think that was what Enoch had in his bottles?" I ask in mock shock.

"Ugh! Abraxx! That was disgusting!"

"Sorry." *Drack.* I've offended her.

She slings her arm around my neck and says, "Between the two of us we've seen a lot of hardships. I want to put that behind me. Please don't be afraid to joke with me. I want far more laughter in my life. We both deserve it."

I pull her across my lap and say, "I want to give you that, Juno. You're right. We both deserve more smiles." I suggestively lift my brow and say, "Perhaps you'll be dancing for me sooner than we anticipated."

"And perhaps for more than fifteen minutes at a time." She's even more beautiful when she smiles.

Chapter Seven

Juno

We sit in silence for a while. I could stay here all day. I feel so safe. And cared for. I could get addicted to this.

"We should probably go," Abraxx says without moving to leave.

"Probably," I agree, snuggling closer. I slide my palm across his cheek and touch one of his *brill*. He breathes in sharply as the look in his eyes darkens with passion. Maybe I can coax him into another session of lovemaking.

He must be thinking the same thing because he slowly dips his head toward me signaling he's about to kiss me. Pulling back at the last moment, he says, "I release you from our bargain. I won't be able to share a room with you without wanting to do this again." He brushes his thumb across my lips with a hungry look in his eyes.

"Who said anything about not doing this again?" I ask.

"I don't want you to feel pressured."

"Was there something I said or did in the last few hours that made you think I feel pressured?" To add emphasis to my words, I reach to stroke one of his *brill*. I pluck the tip just the way he likes, feeling as if I've read the beginner's manual for his body and looking forward to the advanced version. He sucks in a quick breath, then grunts.

I feel him harden against my hip and don't hesitate to grip him, straddle him, and place him at my entrance.

"Juno," he breathes in surprise.

As slow and tender as our coupling was before, this time it's hard and fast. He lifts me and steps to the middle of the pool. We're both half in and half out of the water. I'm buoyant enough and he's strong enough that I can ride him even while babying my right ankle.

He lifts me up as if I weigh nothing, then he slams me down on him, never pushing me onto his thick knob, but making me feel fully owned and fully fucked all the same. I love his undiluted joy in the act, the grunts and hisses and groans he makes keeping no secret of how much pleasure he's taking from our coupling.

I steal a move from his playbook, letting loose my own sighs and moans and not restraining my urge to say his name over and over. I moan his name when he bites the tendons on my neck and when he dips that sexy head to nip the tips of my breasts and when he squeezes my ass cheeks with abandon. I don't hold back when I come, spasming around him and screaming his name in the warm echoing chamber.

When we're both spent, I sag onto him, my face nestled against his neck, both hands curled around his thick *brill*.

"Too good," I say at the same time he says, "Making you feel good could become my favorite pastime. No," he pauses, "my life's work."

He twirls us in the water as he hums, reprising his dance from last night.

"You're a bad male," I scold. "How dare you coerce me like that?" I giggle, then kiss him hard.

We use the blanket we brought along to dry off. As we're dressing, I marvel at how my leg feels no pain at all. He helps me pull on my leggings, so my bad leg doesn't have to bear my weight, but it doesn't feel like I need the help. If I hadn't been there when he cracked my bone two nights ago, I'd never know my leg had been broken.

As we leave, we hear the comms before we get to the hover. It's Dawn's voice and she's yelling.

"Come on you two. This isn't funny. I've been hailing you for hours. If you don't answer in the next five minutes, Dhoom's going to look for you."

As urgent as Dawn sounds, Abraxx carries me to my side of the hover and sets me gently in the seat before he grabs the comm.

"Hello. It's Abraxx."

"Are you and Juno okay?" Dawn sounds breathless.

"Yes. Fine."

"No problems?"

"We're fine."

"Then why the fuck haven't you answered your comm? I've been worried sick. I wondered if the *crindles* got you. Or more rustlers."

"I'm not used to wearing my wrist-comm. I left it in my room. Juno hasn't been issued one yet."

"You'd better get your asses back to the compound. Naomi is on the warpath. I've been instructed to tell you to go straight to Naomi's office the moment you arrive."

"I don't want to get you in trouble, Abraxx," I say as soon as the comm is terminated. "I heard your comm with

Naomi that first night. I imagine she's pissed at you and Dawn."

"It's all going to be okay. Surely she has bigger worries, like the *anlak* rustlers."

"What if she kicks me out?" Panic slices down my spine at the thought. As much as I've dreamed of being free all these years, it terrifies me to think of being alone out in this big galaxy. I have no idea how I'd make a living or keep myself safe. My mind spins with questions as I wonder where I'd go and what I'd do.

Abraxx was in the process of taking off, but he sets the hover on the ground, reaches over, and grabs my hand.

"I'll take care of you Juno. No matter what happens. I have skills. You do, too. If we don't have the safety of Sanctuary, we'll find another way. I'm responsible for you now."

The situation is absurd. I met this man two days ago. Yet I have feelings for him, and they seem to be returned. I don't doubt his veracity when he says he'll be there for me. I think I'd like that.

After I bring his hand to my lips for a brief kiss, he takes off and hovers us back to the heart of the compound. He parks in the hangar, then lifts me onto his back to carry me to Naomi's office.

"I can walk on my own," I tell him.

"I don't doubt that, but perhaps Naomi would feel more forgiving if she doesn't know you can."

"Smart man."

Dhoom meets us in the hangar and blocks our way. He's a scary-looking fucker. Abraxx said all the males used to be gladiators, and I can certainly imagine he was good at what he did. He's taller than Abraxx and bulky with thick muscles. His skin is light with dark swirling patterns over most of it, and I can see almost all of it because all he's wearing is a loincloth.

But it's his horns, black as night, and deadly sharp that are the scariest part of him. No, that's not true, perhaps it's his glowing eyes, the color of embers, or his long top-knot of matching-color hair.

I wonder if Fairea has the death penalty and if he's considering performing it. His face is tight and angry as if he's grinding his molars.

"I'm glad I caught you, brother," he says to Abraxx, his voice calm and warm. "Juno," he nods to me as an introduction. "Naomi is angry. I've tried to run interference, but she wants Juno gone. She's going to come at you with everything she's got, but rest assured I'll do whatever I can to keep you here."

By the look of him, I would have laid even odds that he wanted to grind my bones to dust. But he's friendly and has an amiable relationship with Abraxx. That just reminds me not to judge a book by its cover.

"I've gotten to know her over these last few weeks," he says. "She lives in a place of fear, not evil. She means well. We'll weather this."

Abraxx and Dhoom jog to Naomi's office in the low-slung building in the heart of the compound. The stark looks on both their faces isn't reassuring.

"Come," Naomi barks when Abraxx knocks on her door. Her office is as big as a school classroom and decked out like the poshest office I've ever seen. The walls are paneled in burled wood, and the desk is almost as big as a Ping-Pong table.

The room is lined with hand-crafted shelves made of the chestnut and rose-colored wood that match the compound's structures. I get the feeling that the curios on every shelf aren't just pretty, but are probably priceless. I assume they're artifacts from Daneur Khour's tenure here.

Naomi is forty, maybe older, with brown hair pulled into a loose bun. She's all business and wears her anger and disdain like armor.

Naomi speaks into her comm. "Dawn, you need to get in here, too. Now."

Shit. I hadn't wanted to get anyone in trouble, but I imagine Dawn isn't being called in here to receive a commendation.

After Dawn enters and is ordered to sit, Naomi begins.

"I'm Naomi. I'm in charge of the females in Sanctuary. This is Dhoom; he's in charge of the males. We took over this compound about a month ago and are still trying to find our asses with both hands.

"Job number one is to keep this place running. We need to buy more livestock, plant crops, and figure out how to make money when right now we're hemorrhaging credits setting things up. After yesterday, we've added a new concern to the growing list—cattle rustlers and hillbilly rapists. You'd think we stepped back in time to the Old West. We're going to have to add better surveillance and reinforce the existing fencing.

"We thought down the road this might become a place of refuge for human slaves."

She spears Dawn and Abraxx with a frigid look, then says, "That was to be *down the road*. *Far* down the road. When we could afford more mouths to feed. And there was never a plan for us to gallivant around *buying* human women. Dawn, what made you think you had permission to distribute Sanctuary funds?"

"Umm, I . . ." Dawn stutters.

"Don't even bother answering," Naomi scolds. Her mouth has been a firm line since we arrived, now it has tightened into an angry frown.

She turns to me and says, "I'm sorry, Juno. The credits used to buy you were not authorized. I meant to catch you first thing yesterday, but spent the better part of the day cleaning up the mess the rustlers made, including overseeing burial detail. I'm glad we only buried their dead, not ours.

"It's too late to get the credits back that we spent on you, but I'm afraid we can't afford to keep you." Frankly, she doesn't look sorry at all.

At this point, Dhoom interrupts, speaking directly to Naomi, "What's done is done. She's here. Let's put her to use and move on."

From the furious look on his devilish face, I thought he was figuring out how to barbeque me and eat me for dinner. It's a relief to know he's reserved his rage for Naomi. For the life of me, I can't figure out which one of them is angrier.

"Everyone here needs to know this isn't allowed," Naomi continues as if no words just came out of Dhoom's mouth. "We can't afford another mistake like this." She turns to me and says, "We'll hover you back to the fairgrounds. I'm sure you can find another way to support yourself."

"Support myself? You mean you're sure some other asshole will see a vulnerable single female and slap a slave collar around my neck. Perhaps my new master will actually feed me. You're human? You've been a slave? How can you do this?"

I didn't realize it, but as I was reaming her a new asshole I got up, paced to the front of her enormous desk, and am leaning over it. My face is inches from hers. When I realize my position, although a bolt of terror flies up my spine, I don't retreat or hurry back to my chair.

"I thought your leg was broken," is all she says.

"It was," I say without breaking eye contact. I don't understand how she could cast me out when she's been in this same situation herself. I'm so angry it feels like fire ants are biting me under my skin. It's as if my body is on fire from the inside out.

"I'll take her," Abraxx says calmly. "I'll pack my belongings and we'll be ready to leave within an *hoara*. Dhoom, can you hover us to the fair? We'll find our way from there. I owe the compound a debt of three thousand credits and will be true to my promise. When Juno and I can afford it, we'll send a bit at a time. Let's go, Juno."

"You can't go, Abraxx!" Naomi shouts as she rises from her chair. "What about the twenty bags of *drassah* seeds the compound bought?"

"Someone else can plant them," he says. "Come on, Juno."

"Sit down!" Naomi thunders when we both turn to leave. Neither of us make a move to return to our chairs but we stop walking and hold her angry gaze.

"You said you were raised on a *drassah* plantation," Naomi protests. "That you were taught from an early age how to cultivate the land, raise the crops, and pick the ripest fruit. I've been lucky enough to have a cup of *drassah* every time I sat down with Daneur Khour to plan how I would best serve him. It's better than coffee. Which means it's the best-tasting morning beverage in the galaxy.

"It was only because of your experience that we purchased twenty bags of seeds and committed 211 *rextans* of land to a *drassah* crop. I'm told only the most experienced cultivators in the galaxy can tell a ripe bean from one that's past its prime. No one else in the compound can grow these things. You have to stay."

"Juno and I are a package. We both stay or we leave together." He's risking everything to protect me. My heart swells with gratitude.

For the briefest moment, I see what his opponents must have seen when they faced him in the gladiatorial arena. I'm glad I've never observed this expression before. It's hard and strong, his eyes slit in anger. I never want to be on the receiving end of that. I'm glad it's directed at Naomi.

"Shit. We've spent 927 credits per *rextan* for 211 *rextans*. No one but you has the expertise to make this work." She drops back into her seat and inspects the burls as if the answers to the mysteries of the universe are written in code in the whorls of the wood.

"You've got 195,597 credits riding on this project and you're willing to throw it away to punish him for spending 3,000?" I ask, incredulous.

Her angry gray gaze flies to me and flicks up and down as if she's seeing me for the first time. She punches something into her wrist-comm and then looks at me, one eyebrow raised in question.

"How did you know what 927 times 211 is?"

"Numbers come easy to me." I shrug.

"People need calculators for numbers like that. I checked it. Twice. Your computation was correct."

Abraxx places his warm hand on the small of my back and escorts me toward the door.

"Stop! You two are officially invited to stay. Abraxx, I'd like you to remain here to oversee the *drassah* planting and production. Juno, if you stay you will become our accountant."

"I know nothing about accounting," I say. I'm not certain I want to take her up on her offer.

"Accounting can be taught. Having a mind for figures can't be learned. You have a gift."

Maybe Naomi has multiple personalities, because she's like a different person. Her shoulders aren't high and tight like they had been, and the features of her face are softer, prettier.

"Can we put our heads together?" Abraxx asks. Funny, he's using the same phrase I did when we were negotiating with Enoch.

We slip into the hallway to discuss her offer. It doesn't take long. It turns out neither of us was particularly excited about leaving Sanctuary with no money, no transportation, and no plan.

When we return to Naomi's office, neither of us takes a seat.

"Naomi," Abraxx says, looking at her pointedly, "you owe Juno an apology."

She takes a deep breath, then shutters her eyes for a moment as if she's having an internal debate.

"You're right. I owe . . ." She pauses and scrapes her top lip with her bottom teeth as she appears to gear up to say whatever's next. "I owe everyone here an apology."

She's been standing, every muscle in her body tense as we argued, now she settles back into her chair and puts her palms on her desk.

"There isn't a soul in this compound who hasn't had a hard life. We were all slaves. Everyone in this room experienced their own version of hell. We all cope in different ways. Some people break, some get stronger. Taking control makes me feel less vulnerable."

I've only known Naomi for a few minutes, but I imagined her backbone was made of granite, her nerves of steel, and I figured her chest was devoid of a heart. Her admission of weakness astonishes me. Looking at the stunned expressions on everyone's faces in the room, I'm not the only one.

"I need to remind myself we're all working toward the same thing." She glances down for a moment, then looks back at us. "We all want safety, security, and maybe a modicum of happiness. You two are welcome to stay. I'm sorry for being harsh.

"Perhaps it's no excuse, but I feel personally responsible for every person in this compound. I worry about having enough money to get through the winter. I worry about finding the funds to buy armaments for when Khour's successor shows up wondering how we own this property when no funds were transferred. I worry *constantly* for the greater good of us all. I just want us all to be safe." She gives Abraxx and me a stare and a nod, smiles apologetically at Dawn, then pegs Dhoom with a serious look she can't maintain as her gaze runs back to the top of her desk.

Now that we're not worried we're going to be banished from Sanctuary, Dawn looks at me and says, "I saw your ankle yesterday. It was swollen and all shades of bruised. I heard Pherutan say you needed to stay off it for several days. How are you able to walk on it now without the brace?"

"We found a cave with a natural hot spring in a good size pool. Abraxx and I soaked in it for at least an hour and when I emerged my leg was as good as new."

Naomi's brow raises in interest and she stands, leaning over her desk to inspect me. "Healed? I'll have Pherutan look into it. It could be another income stream."

I stifle a laugh. She's nothing if not consistent. It's very apparent Naomi wants to make certain we all have a safe place to live and enough food to eat.

Abraxx

When we were out in the hallway a moment ago, I had mixed feelings about whether to stay or leave. I know it's safer for Juno if we remain here, that's why I voted for it. But no one wants to remain where they're resented, or not wanted altogether.

Now that Naomi has apologized, the decision to stay feels right. I grew up playing in the family *drassah* fields.

From a young age, my father taught me the best time to plant, how to tell which day the beans were perfectly ripe, and how to coax more production from each bush. I love everything about *drassah* from the plants themselves to the reward of a rich cup of *drassah* with cream to begin each morning.

On Numa, we're taught we are born with a *brumah*, something we're born to do. Most people have to wait years to discover theirs, I've known mine my whole life. I never wanted to be a gladiator. I was born to work the *drassah* fields. I can't wait to start planting.

I knew Juno was a gifted dancer but was shocked at how her mind calculates numbers like a computer. It sounds as if numbers, not dancing, is her *brumah*.

"Will you be happy working with numbers in an office?" I ask after we leave Naomi's office. I would hate it. I always loved being outdoors all day with the plants. My imprisonment in an underground dungeon didn't make me any fonder of being indoors.

"I love numbers. Always have. On Earth, our vehicles had license plates. There's something about numbers that makes them stick in my head. Every license plate I passed would stay in my memory. My brain was full of them until I taught myself the trick of washing my mind of them every evening. At bedtime, I'd picture myself dumping all the license plates into the dishwasher and the next morning my mind would be empty and start accumulating them again. Weird, huh?"

"No. Not weird. It works?" We were walking toward the exit, but I stop in my tracks and grab her hand. "You wash away things in your mind and they disappear?" I urgently want an answer.

"I don't have a dishwasher in my head. It's just . . . my imagination helped the numbers go away."

"Do you think it will work for me? For what happened in the dungeon?" I ask.

"Hmmm." She thinks. "Or me, for all the days of my captivity? I never thought of it."

I don't know what a dishwasher is, but I can imagine washing my memories in the stream near my house on Numa.

"I'm going to try it tonight," I tell her. "Right after I make you moan again."

She glances at the floor. My words made her shy, but I think she liked them.

"No. Maybe right after you scream in pleasure."

She smiles and peeks at me through her lashes.

"No. Maybe after I taste you." I pause until she glances at me. "So many choices, Juno. Which do you want?"

"All of them, Abraxx. Every. Single. One."

"But you're going to sleep in your own room. We've got time now. We're going to stay at Sanctuary. We have all the time we need to get to know each other better."

"I want to stay with you in your room." She steps close and places her palms on my chest.

"And I you. But I want you to have choices. I want you to be able to get to know the other females and get to know me. Besides, you can keep your original bargain." I glance down, reminding us both that she's walking on her own two feet without any help from me. "I'm going to feed you, then take you to my room and watch you dance."

Two Months Later

Juno

If the fortune teller in the booth across from where I used to dance had told me that in the span of two months I would get a fabulous new career that made me feel fulfilled and valuable, I would have called her a liar. If she'd told me I'd find a new family who loved me as much as my Earth family, I would have called her crazy. And if she'd predicted I'd be freed and fall in love with the galaxy's sexiest, handsomest, kindest male, I would have called her psychotic. And yet all of that has come to pass since my late-night arrival at the Sanctuary compound.

Most surprising of all? How much Abraxx loves me. I don't doubt it's true, though. He tells me a dozen times a day, but words have never meant much to me. Words can lie. It's the way he shows me in a thousand different ways, and the look in his ice-blue eyes when he gazes at me like he's doing right now that proves his love is real.

"Nervous, Love?" he asks, his head cocked in question.

"No. I've never been more certain about anything in my life."

"Nor I, Juno." He crosses the space between us and plants a soft kiss on my forehead. He told me it's a blessing of love in his culture. I cherish those kisses. "Dhoom and I need a moment alone, love."

I wonder if this has anything to do with the secret he's been keeping from me for the past month. There has been a lot of whispering and late nights and early mornings where he has urgent things to do on the other side of the property. I trust him implicitly though. And there's no reason to worry. Not today of all days.

"I'll be in my room in the mansion, Abraxx. Comm me when you're ready."

Abraxx

These next moments with Dhoom are going to be bittersweet. I've had fifteen *annums* to accept the fact that the day the invaders stole me, they razed our house, farm, and crops and killed my family. You'd think I would have had plenty of time to mourn, but I still miss them.

A male gets his first *sygnet* on the eighteenth anniversary of his birth. It is made and placed on his most prominent *brill* by his father. My abductors stole that honor from me. I explained this to Dhoom, showed him pictures of various *sygnets* on the Intergalactic Database, and told him I would be privileged if he would do the honors.

Out of all the males in the dungeon, he and I forged a bond, that is until we became too weak and disheartened to converse.

I didn't think he would refuse my request, but I never imagined he would take his duties so seriously. He's spent weeks researching the *sygnet*, designing, fashioning, and polishing it. He's prepared for the personal ceremony that usually includes only father and son. When he knocks and enters my room, he looks more anxious than I am.

He's filled out in the *lunars* since our release. He'd been one of the most debilitated of the males in the dungeon. He spent his own credits to hire a tailor from the village to make him a fine suit that represents the regalia his race wear to their most sacred ceremonies. It's a tunic that covers his chest and splits at the waist so slits ride along the outside of his legs from his hips to his sandal-covered feet.

"Abraxx, I'm honored to be in the position of a beloved father," his voice breaks with emotion. We became close during our time underground, and even closer since our release, but I sense there's something more going on than our friendship. "I have given thought to the *sygnet* design that signifies your passage from youngling to grown male. In your culture, it represents a time to put away the thoughts and feelings of a child and turn to the responsibilities of an adult.

"You've been of age for a long time, so let this *sygnet* also represent turning away from the past and facing the future. May your fate be bright and filled with happiness and love."

He pulls the *sygnet* out of a pouch in the front of his ceremonial tunic, cups it in his palm, and shows it to me.

It's delicately made, the *hoaras* of fine workmanship are obvious even at first glance. It's composed of many small golden circles. The circle is sacred to my people because it signifies no beginning and no ending, the endless cycle of life.

"May your life be filled with love and blessings, Abraxx. I've had the opportunity to watch you during our time in the dungeon. Those were black days, and I hate to remind you of them, but a males' character is forged in times like those, and you emerged with your dignity and your ability to love intact. A lesser male might have become angry and hardened." His jaw works for a while, but no words are spoken. Is he indicating he emerged from his cell as less of a male? I have nothing but respect for him.

"I place this on you as a rite of passage. You are a full-fledged and accepted member of the tribe. *Our* tribe, the Sanctuary tribe."

He respectfully grips my thickest, longest *brill* and slides the *sygnet* up until it lodges as high as it will go.

"May this be the first of many *sygnets* that represent the highlights of a long and happy life." He clasps my upper arms in his palms and dips his head to me in affection and respect.

"Thank you, Dhoom. You have no idea how much this means to me."

"I'm honored you included me in this sacred rite."

Juno

My wrist-comm startles me when it vibrates, even though I was expecting it. Abraxx must have completed his business and is ready for me.

"Is it time?" Dawn asks. "You look beautiful, and it's going to be the best wedding ever," she says with a brilliant smile.

"I admit, I'm freaking."

"He's a wonderful male, and he loves you. I get jealous every time I see him looking at you like you hung the moon. Well . . . moons."

I glance in the mirror and smooth my dress. It's been a labor of love for the women in the compound. We've all worked on it, and Dawn's right, it looks good on me. She's brushed my blonde hair to a high gloss and helped me apply makeup that makes my brown eyes pop. I shouldn't have let her do the makeup, though, I have a feeling I'm going to cry and make it run.

Melodie knocks tentatively and enters with a huge bouquet of wildflowers. "I've spent the last hour picking these near the river's edge. Have you ever seen anything like them?"

She's standoffish, or maybe she's shy. She and Thran do secret jobs off this planet she's not allowed to talk about. Perhaps that's why she keeps to herself and seldom joins the women for our gossip- and giggle-fests.

She holds the flowers under my nose and the sweetest fragrance drifts to me.

"The ones that look like purple stars smell the best. I want to learn how to bottle that. Yummy, right?"

"Divine," I answer. "Whatever they are could definitely be made into the galaxy's best perfume."

"I've decided that's exactly what I'm going to do. I've been looking for a way to help out other than going on Naomi's errands. I'm going to learn to make perfume now that Thran and I are mated."

"I know you've only been mated a short while, but . . . how does it feel?"

I'm pretending to be my normal self, but I can't hide the fact that my hands are trembling. This is the most important day of my life.

"Better than you can imagine," Melodie says with a reassuring smile.

"We've got you," Dawn says, grabbing one of my hands as Melodie grips the other. A few minutes later we've crossed the courtyard, passed the well and the scar in the soil that reminds us where our males were held captive underground.

The three of us are standing outside the sanctuary. We've discovered a lot in the last few months. We were right when we surmised this used to be the heart of a feudal town. The castle still stands, we call it the mansion. The old well is still here, and this was the original temple.

At first, it wasn't high on the list of buildings to rehabilitate, but when Abraxx asked me to be his mate, it moved to the top of the priority list. We've swept it out, righted pews that had fallen over in disrepair, and repainted.

Melodie's been busy. The flowers in my bouquet aren't the only ones she picked. The room is filled with baskets and vases full of them. I'll never catch a whiff of the purple starflowers again without being reminded of my mating day.

Abraxx is standing at the front of the room with Dhoom behind him ready to perform the ceremony. I see a *sygnet* on one of his *brill*. Although it's lovely, it's not as beautiful as the one in my gown's hidden pocket. I'm certain it wasn't made with as much love, either.

Although I don't want to tear my eyes from my beloved, I take the opportunity to look at each of my new friends.

Willa and Bayne are here, holding hands in one of the pews. They stayed on Fairea after coming to fight Khour. It's no secret Bayne, in his canine shifter form, ended Khour's life and found the imprisoned gladiators hidden in the underground cages.

When Abraxx told me Bayne could shift into a huge canine, it explained the canine I saw the day the rustlers attacked that appeared as if by magic. The couple is held in high esteem, but I think everyone will forever hold a special debt of gratitude to Bayne for killing the male who made all our lives a living hell.

I'm glad to see So'Lan here, so I give him my widest smile. He was the most damaged of all the males who were carried out of that dungeon three months ago. No one thought he would live. He's still weak and underweight, but he's filled out a bit since I first met him, and his face looks more like a lion every day. I think the regular soaks in the hot spring we discovered have helped. I look forward to the time his eyes don't show evidence of how hard his life was. It would be wonderful if one day he finds love as pure as Abraxx and I.

I feel a bit sad Naomi is sitting alone in a pew. She's softened since that awful day in her office when she threatened to throw me out of Sanctuary. She keeps sneaking glances at Dhoom at the front of the room. They say it's a thin line between love and hate, but by the decibel level of the arguments I hear when I walk past her door, I think their line is pretty thick. And angry. And irreparable.

Of course, everyone else in the compound is here, but now it's time for the ceremony. As I stand by his side, I inspect my male. Instead of his usual blue *sha'rill*, he's wearing a silky one the prettiest shade of pale sunshine yellow. Best of all, it doesn't cover his face. I think he finally feels like he belongs here and no longer has to hide.

His facial expression is calm and loving, but he can't fool me, his tail is flicking from side to side under the hem of his *sha'rill* like an anxious feline. When I tear my eyes from his handsome face and pay attention, I notice Dhoom's words are solemn and optimistic. My attention though is on how perfect a couple Abraxx and I are, and how our love has grown as we've gotten to know each other.

"It's time for the *sygnet*," Abraxx whispers. I pull out the piece of golden jewelry I've been working on for weeks. I watched dozens of hours of what passes for YouTube videos on the Intergalactic Database and I think I did a fine job with the thin strands of gold wire Dhoom donated to the cause.

"Let this *sygnet* be forever a reminder of how our love is inextricably entwined. I designed it so the top band represents you, the bottom band represents me, and they are forever linked together," I tell him solemnly.

He kneels in front of me, and I grip the same *brill* that now wears another adornment. After sliding it as far up as it will go, I tell him, "I love you more than words can say, my love."

He stands and sincerely says, "I love you more than words can say," as he places a thin gold band on my ring finger.

Someone must have explained Earth customs to Dhoom because he intones, "Now you two may kiss."

We share a soft, sweet, heartfelt kiss in front of the assembly as they cheer and clap and the males stomp their feet. The hot look we exchange makes it clear we'll be experiencing many more when we get back to the room we've agreed to share in the mansion.

For some reason, in the press of happy people wishing us a long, loving union, Abraxx asked me to wait at the sanctuary door with Dawn and Melodie.

"You're going to love it!" Dawn says, her eyes alight with excitement.

"It's perfect," Melodie says, a wide smile on her face.

"What are you talking about?"

"We figured you had to know by now. We've barely been able to keep the secret," Melodie says.

Thran approaches us. I'm told the muscular, handsome male always seemed melancholy, like he'd never truly been freed from that dungeon before he met Melodie. He seems calm and happy now.

"I hope you love your new lodging, Juno. We all worked hard to make it a wonderful place to raise a family."

He's so earnest I don't want to let him know he just spilled the beans and spoiled the secret.

"I know I will, Thran. I'm certain you helped make it special."

The three of us women don't breathe a word until he walks away.

"Tell me. Tell me right now," I demand.

"Here's your new mate," Melodie says. "There's still a lot to be surprised about."

Abraxx pulls up to the mansion door on one of the hover-sleds we appropriated from the rustlers. It's been repainted and titled to Sanctuary at what I'm told is no small expense.

We all know not to ask too many questions about where the money's coming from. One day Naomi cries poor and we wonder if there's going to be enough to eat, the next day one of the women returns from what we're told is a 'vacation' and we have enough credits to buy big-ticket items like new farming equipment or to repair the shiny hover-sleds.

The fire-engine red machine Abraxx's fine ass is sitting on looks like a cross between a motorcycle and a jet ski. I tell the women goodbye, climb behind him, and we hover off.

"I have a surprise for you," Abraxx says as he reaches back to pat my knee. "We're not going to share a room in the mansion. I've already had all your things moved to the cottage."

The cottage is an adorable structure at the edge of the lower forty. It's not really the lower forty, it's actually the lower two-hundred-eleven. But all the women have seen enough old western TV shows that we like to call it that. It borders the *drassah* field.

I helped Abraxx plant the field with care, and now it's burgeoning with perfect rows of verdant green bushes. Abraxx tells me that in a few months, they'll be full of bright red berries that will become the best *drassah* in the quadrant. I've never drunk *drassah*, but the leaves are fragrant and sweet as perfume.

I hug Abraxx's waist. He's put on a few pounds over the last months. After being starved during his stay in the compound's dungeon, he's now at his preferred weight. I'm not picky; I've always thought he was the most handsome male I've ever seen.

I move his *brill* to kiss the exposed flesh of his nape, and my lips curl into a smile as I remember that first night I saw him. I'd danced for Enoch for years but had never taken notice of any male in the audience. I'd learned long ago they were all assholes. I certainly never parted a sea of patrons, grabbed a male's hand, and pulled him to the stage to dance with me.

Abraxx and I were simply meant to be together. Some part deep in my soul must have known it the first moment I saw him.

For the first month we were together, I worried that our attraction wasn't real. At first, I attributed it to the way he touched me. He was sweet and tender and the nicest person I've met since I left Earth. Then I wondered if it was the sex because, well, when we touch it's incendiary.

We kept our bargain. I danced for him every night for thirty days. The original agreement was to dance alone in his room, and that's what I did. Every night he picked a different piece of music from the Intergalactic Database.

Some were slow, some fast, some lyrical, and some could barely be considered music. But I danced my heart out for that male partly because for the first time in years I was dancing of my own free will, and partly because of the rapt look of attention on his face. Well, and maybe partly because by the end of the allotted time his cock was hard as steel beneath his loincloth.

After the fifteen minutes of dancing, we danced together beneath the sheets. The sex has been amazing. It just keeps getting better as we discover new ways to please each other. But the pillow talk afterward has been equally profound. We've shared everything—the good, the bad, and the ugly. Considering we were both slaves for a long time, there was a lot of ugly.

Perhaps it was the act of sharing our secrets, or maybe it was the washing technique we developed where we learned to let everything go, but the past seems solidly behind us now.

I squeeze Abraxx tighter as we approach the cottage. It, like every other structure in the compound, is made in the same style, with blocks of rose and chestnut-colored stone. It's obvious that various artisans worked on the structures over centuries, but they all maintain the same checkerboard pattern, whimsical lines with arched doorways, and fanciful rooflines.

Our cottage looks to be one of the oldest buildings in the compound. I fell in love with its fairytale roofline and asymmetrical windows that made the house look like something out of <u>Hansel and Gretel</u>, or maybe <u>The Hobbit</u>.

The last time I was in here it was full of dead leaves and mummified rodents. The roof had developed leaks long ago, and the floorboards beneath were ruined. All I needed to say was how quaint the cottage was, though, and that it was too bad it had fallen into disrepair. Abraxx must have started working on renovations right away.

I'll admit, I knew something was up because I haven't been allowed inside since the day Abraxx and I discovered it.

"You're going to love it," he calls over his shoulder as he stops the hover and it lowers to the ground. "The males have been helping since I started, then I enlisted the women for finishing touches. There isn't a person in the compound who hasn't put their stamp on it. Even So'Lan added something. He painted the picture of the exterior of the cottage that's now hanging over the mantle. Well, Naomi didn't actually do any of the physical work, but she did approve the expenses, with only a few grumbles," he says with a chuckle.

"On Numa, the couple is expected to walk through the door together the first time they enter a house. It signifies the equality of the male and female. Although a Numan didn't design this doorway, we can squeeze through if we face each other. That will be good because I can't wait to see the expression on your face when you see your new home for the first time."

The last time I was here, the weeds and brambles had reclaimed both the exterior and interior of this house.

Not only did my friends perform miracles on the inside, but the outside is now manicured.

Abraxx's strong hands hold my waist as we stand outside the door facing each other. Our gazes connect, and we slide through together.

It's only when he asks, "What do you think?" that I tear my eyes from his and inspect the house. It's the perfect cottage—small and charming. There are white curtains at the windows and comfortable furniture in the main room.

The windows, canted at such odd angles, bring whimsy into the house. How could it be possible to fight in a place that looks like this? I half expect one of the chairs to start dancing like something out of <u>Beauty and the Beast.</u>

It's one large space, with a bar separating the kitchen and living area. It seems to be furnished down to pots and pans and cutlery. Down the hallway are a bedroom and bathroom.

"We can add more rooms when you're ready to have a youngling," he says, a happy smile on his handsome, beaming face.

I haven't removed the contraceptive implant I was given the day the slavers slapped the collar on my neck, but Abraxx and I have talked about it. We're not ready yet. We want to enjoy being a couple before we have kids. Pherutan assured us it's possible for humans and Numans to produce offspring.

"I love it. Truly. You couldn't have done better. It's perfect."

"We're here now. This is our home. Naomi's calmed a bit and isn't going to cast us out. She needs me for the *drassah* bushes, and you to help her, what did you call it? Cook the ledgers?"

"Cook the books. You're right. No one's going to force us out. We're mated. You wear my *sygnet*." I look at the male who's so handsome he takes my breath away, then trace my finger along the delicate lines of gold that hug his *brill* as he lifts my left hand and kisses the ring on my finger. "Come, love. Let's go to bed. There's something special I want to try tonight."

He raises a questioning eyebrow but doesn't ask what it is. We'll get there soon enough.

Instead of tearing his *sha'rill* off his perfect body, I urge, "Take your clothes off for me, love."

His blue eyes blaze with passion as he grips the voluminous fabric at his neck.

"I love your *brill*, Abraxx. They're so good to hold onto when we're making love."

"When you do that it never fails to make my cock even harder," he says, his voice gravelly.

His green fingers move to the fabric at his shoulder and unwrap the rest of his *sha'rill* in slow, sexy movements until the garment whispers to the floor. He's in his loincloth now, the material barely containing his sex.

Instead of immediately focusing on the object of my desire, I force my gaze to slide down his body from wide, muscled shoulders to rippled abs until it finally arrives at the cock pulsing in its muslin sling.

"I'm a lucky woman," I say with a smile.

"Show me how lucky *I* am, Juno," he husks as his gaze flicks up and down my body.

I reach behind and touch the auto-zip on the back of my dress. I shimmy, slow and sexy, until the dress slips over one shoulder and eventually slides to pool on the floor.

"I'm a lucky male." He pauses. "Make me even luckier."

I turn to him in the matching bra and panty set I used my first month's wages to buy. The pale pink satin looks good against my tan skin. I've been waiting for tonight to give him this show.

"Lucky. Fortunate. Blessed," he said that last word in a whisper. The expression on his face is adoration. I imagine fifty years from now that look will still make my belly tighten with desire.

When I reach behind to unclasp my bra, he says, "Stop. I'll take it from here." Striding the distance between us, he reaches around me, but before he removes my bra, he bends to kiss my forehead. My bra and panties are soon on the floor and I'm standing naked in our bedroom with only a whisper of air separating us.

Encircling me with his arms, he tugs me even closer and kisses me softly. It's obvious he's trying to go slow, but within moments, the gentle brushing of his kisses transforms into a hard, demanding invasion.

Deep grunts escape from his throat as his tongue plies mine, tasting, stroking, possessing. Cradling the back of my head in his hands, it's as if he doesn't want to release me. He hungers to keep our mouths pressed together forever.

His pulsing cock teases against my midriff. I can't contain myself from releasing it from its cloth prison and gripping its length, loving the silken hardness.

As he lifts me my legs split to encircle his waist.

He pulls his mouth from mine long enough to breathe, "I smell your need, Juno. I'll quench it in a moment. First, though . . ." He dips his head to my nipple and nips the tip just the way he knows will pull a hiss and a moan from me. "First let me make you more needy."

My arms clasp around his neck, my head thrown back in ecstasy as he showers attention on first one hardened bud and then the other. He's rearranged us so his stiff cock presses between us, riding my dripping folds. Or maybe I'm riding him.

For a woman who thought I'd never feel sexual desire again, he's certainly taught me I'm not broken. Not with a male such as Abraxx.

Laying me down on the bed, he holds me just above the knees and splits me open. "Pink is my new favorite color," he says, his voice husky with lust.

"Funny," I tell him, "I'm learning to love green."

He kneels between my thighs and lowers his head as if he's worshipping at an altar.

"I can't wait a moment more to taste you again," he murmurs against my flesh, then dips his tongue into my channel with a guttural moan.

That tongue is relentless as it penetrates deep inside me, then slides out to flick against my hardened nub until my head thrashes against the pillows and I moan. Over and over, he repeats this, ramping my desire higher until I'm desperate.

"I need you," I say. It's somewhere between a demand and a plea.

Instead, he teases me more before he finally slips one finger, then two into my slick channel while he sucks and flicks my clit. His flexible tail is wrapped around my thigh, pinning me wide as if I needed any encouragement to open to him. It tightens around the delicate crease at the top of my thigh which pushes me over the edge of passion. I spasm so hard even my fingers clench as they bite into his thickly muscled shoulders.

Perhaps he never learned about the need for a recovery period, because as soon as my breathing returns to normal, his tongue and fingers assault me again. My mouth is dry from panting, my sighs sound distant in my ears, and my body responds to his as if he's a puppet master in complete command of my pleasure. And pleasure me he does.

Three orgasms later, every muscle quivering, I'm so spent I don't have the energy to cuddle him when he lies next to me and gathers me in his arms.

"Do you think the cottage is magic?" I finally ask when I can command my lips to speak. "Things have never been this good between us." I'm too tired to keep my eyes open while I listen to his response.

"Not the cottage, Juno. It's us. We're magic together."

I have to reward those sweet words with my gaze, no matter how tired I am.

"You're amazing," I say as I turn on my side and cup his cheek in my palm. As I gather my second wind, I tell him,

"I promised you something different. I guess you're wondering what it is."

"I figured we'd get there, love."

I use my small store of energy to lean and kiss those plump green lips as a reward for calling me that. It feels warm and comforting.

"Let's start here," I say as I grip his cock and skate my fingers along his smooth skin, enjoying the journey from the root, over the bulb, past the column of bumps, to the three prominent ridges. He sucks in a sharp breath, which is so sexy it infuses me with energy.

Using one finger, I press his shoulder onto the bed. He was lying on his side but is now on his back. I crawl between his legs and tighten my grip on him, still stroking from base to tip and back again.

His cock is foreign and green and gorgeous. Most of the flesh is emerald green, but the pretty ridges are almost chartreuse.

"How'd you get such a sexy cock?" I ask before I open my mouth to breathe hot air on the head. I love the way it kicks in my hand. I hold his gaze as I dip my head over him with infinite languor. Out of the corner of my eye, I see him grip the sheets as he waits, then hear his appreciative hiss when I take him in my mouth.

"Juno," he says on a groan.

I lick circles around the head, then lower, using the tip of my tongue to trace the pattern of the three hard ridges that provide me so much pleasure when he's pounding into me.

I know I'm doing my job well when he can't control his urge to thrust, his hips making little micro-movements as the sound of his pants gets harsher.

I swallow him, my lips providing pressure as I go as far down his shaft as I can manage. His hands lodge in my hair as he whispers praises. Sometimes I can understand the words, like when he says my name, or "so good," or "perfect." Sometimes it's just quiet murmurings, the meaning of which I can't catch except to hear how much he's enjoying my ministrations.

His breathing is so ragged, I know he won't be able to last long if I continue what I'm doing, so I pull off him slowly, tonguing him in little flicks until he's no longer contained in the warmth of my mouth.

"I want you all the way inside me tonight, Abraxx." I'm not sure he heard me, he's so deep in a lust-filled haze it takes his brain a while to comprehend me. When he does, his gaze flashes to mine.

"I'm too big. What we do is more than any male could hope for."

"If I'm big enough for a baby, I'm big enough for you," I tell him flatly.

Since I've been with Abraxx, I haven't been able to decide which I enjoy more—the instant of entry, the joy of being filled, or the act of sex itself. It's his love, the comfort we have together, than eclipses all my history and allows me to relax and enjoy it all. There's something about the moment when he enters me, though, of when I go from being alone to being connected that is magical.

I place him at my entrance and ease down on him in tiny pulses as he grips my hips. Wordlessly, we gaze at each other. There's something almost sacred about our joining. I want to complete it today. We've never pushed past the bulb on his cock. I want to do this. To complete the connection we've had since we first laid eyes on each other.

I'm slick from arousal and my releases, so I slide onto him easily until I reach his knot.

"Stop if you want, love. I don't need this from you. We're two different species."

"I don't want to stop," I say as I pulse up and down with his knob at my entrance. It's big against me, and there's a moment I'm certain no amount of battering is going to accomplish the task. But I relax, reminding myself how much I love this male and that I want to experience everything there is with him.

That does the trick as I force myself lower onto him. The stretch and burn are delicious and scary, and profane and sacred at the same time. When my gaze flashes to his and I see the look of ecstasy on his face, it makes the discomfort worth it.

I had been riding him upright, but I lean over his chest, place my hands on the bed near his shoulders and begin the slow slide up and then down his shaft again. After one or two trips like this, it no longer feels like he's too big for me. Our connection feels just right.

I roll us, first onto our sides, then with me on my back.

"Love me, Abraxx."

He's gazing at me with awe. How can a woman not love a male who looks at her like that?

He thrusts long and slow, watching my face with each movement, making certain he doesn't hurt me. After a minute of this, he pounds into me in earnest. He's possessing me. I love this feeling, this connection.

Abraxx

She's so beautiful. Her cheeks, usually pink, are flushed with passion. She tries to keep her eyes focused on me, but when the pleasure becomes too intense, her lids shutter, her head tips back, and she swims deep in the pool of passion.

I love this female. We have such an intimate connection. I still can't believe she returns my love. And this? This transcendent experience is beyond physical pleasure, it's divine and luminous.

Her moan and short little pants have transformed into the long, low animal sounds that indicate she's close. I watch her, pacing myself, wanting more than anything to join her at the moment of her bliss.

When her channel spasms around me, her mouth is a perfect 'o'. The pressure on my bulb is exquisite. I had no idea the bliss of our previous lovemaking could reach this level of sublime pleasure. I soar to the stars as I permit my own release. My balls tingle, and I allow myself to jet into her, to claim her, to make her mine.

The moment I quit spasming, I tell her, "I love you," as I watch her back arch off the bed in ecstasy.

As she floats back from wherever she goes when her mind is consumed with pleasure, I slide onto the bed next to her and cover her face with kisses.

"I'm a lucky male," I tell her. "The luckiest day of my life was the day I met you. The luckiest moment of my life was when you pushed through the crowd to make your way to me. The best *minima* of my life was when you agreed to be my mate. We're going to make a good life together."

Juno

It thrills me that he knows how lucky we are that we found each other. I love being at Sanctuary. I have my Abraxx. Our mating was beautiful and sacred. We've both found jobs that make us feel useful and competent.

We have this wonderful cottage where I know we'll experience many joys together. When I picture raising little Abraxxes or a little girl with blond hair, brown eyes, and green skin, it fills my heart with delight.

How amazing is it that they even named this place Sanctuary? It's the perfect word. We've all experienced a lot of pain in this cold, harsh galaxy, yet we found safety and friendship and yes, even love.

Sanctuary, indeed.

The End

Dear Readers,

I hope you enjoyed this book. Abraxx and Juno's love was so sweet I wanted to share it with you. WANT EVEN MORE? I've written a second epilogue that will fog your e-readers even more than the last chapter. Abraxx's tail finally gets all the way into the action. Contact me by email at alanakhanauthor@gmail.com and ask for Abraxx's reader magnet. It will wing its way to you the moment I open your email.

Curious about Dawn? She gets her happily ever after in book 3 of the series—Revikk. After everything she did to help Abraxx and Juno, she deserves to find love too, right?

Here's her Sneak Peek. But first, let me ask you to review Abraxx. Reviews are so important to independent authors like myself. They help people decide to buy my books, which allows me to keep writing. Thanks!

Revikk: Book Three of the Galaxy Sanctuary Alien Abduction Romance Series

Planet Fairea
Present Day

Dawn

Today's the day. I'm going to sleep with the leather guy. A year ago, my behavior would have scandalized me. Today, after what I've endured, I feel entitled to it. I deserve some pleasure after all I've been through, don't I?

I was kidnapped from my bed in Georgia and have been in outer space for a year. Yeah, I know, time flies when you're having fun.

Actually, I have no idea how long I've been gone. I was drugged and in stasis for a while on the trip here. I could be one hundred instead of twenty for all I know. I'll stick with twenty, it's not as scary.

A male named Daneur Khour, head of the biggest crime syndicate in the galaxy and in charge of most human abductions, had me brought directly to his compound on planet Fairea.

I was told he was handsome in his day, but by the time I was literally slung onto the floor at his feet, one of his enemies had done a number on his face. I'm here to attest that acid and flesh do not mix well. His face looked like it had been churned by a mixmaster and then melted.

That was the beginning of my conviction that I'm a hell of a lot stronger than I ever believed. It took every ounce of strength I had to look that motherfucker right in the eye as if he was as pretty as Jason Momoa.

Perhaps there was something about me he didn't like, because he took a hard pass on partaking of my sexual favors. My hypothesis is that the psychopath enjoyed forcing sex on people he could repulse. It was as if forcing himself on a disgusted innocent turned him on even more than other non-consensual sex. Since he didn't have that effect on me, I was no fun.

I'll never know the whys of it, but he had me tossed into the female dormitory at his compound and never called me to his bedroom again. Nor did he put me to any other use. I was just warehoused for nine months. Not that I'm complaining.

I'll say one thing. I've been a big believer in the Almighty since the day Khour kicked me out of his bedroom.

Three months ago, some gladiators invaded his compound, killed his grotesque, psychotic ass, and set me free along with four other women in the dorm. They also freed eight gladiators Khour had stashed in some underground hellhole as punishment for real or imagined infractions.

Through some not-quite-legal sleight-of-hand, we now own the compound. We're just a bunch of former slaves trying to find our asses with both hands as we figure out how to keep the place running.

We named the compound Sanctuary and hope to someday take in refugees who've escaped slavery. Of course, all of us human women are picturing it being a safe haven for other human women.

The spread covers thousands of acres. In addition to housing the mansion and a gladiator arena, there are outbuildings galore as well as barns and single-family dwellings.

As soon as we took possession, we decided we had to become self-sufficient. Some of us began to farm the land, others took responsibility for the herd of *anlaks* we bought. They're basically ugly, four-eyed cows.

Some cook, or work on the books, and a few go on super-secret 'missions' that sound shady as hell but bring in the money we desperately need to keep the operation going.

I put myself in charge of the chicken-like animals that were already roaming the property. I grew up on a little farm in Georgia. Our eight acres grew produce, goats, and chickens. Our place was called a truck farm because we trucked everything we grew and raised to the city to sell at fairs.

I saw the pretty *prens* preening and walking around like they owned the place and figured raising them was how I could earn my keep.

For the past eight weeks, I've brought fresh eggs to the fair every other day. I've been resourceful: I found a booth that sells fresh fruit and vegetables. The owner was happy to buy our eggs wholesale and sell them at retail.

It's not an exaggeration to say that over the last two months I've become addicted to the fair. It's an hour east of our compound and more interesting than any place I ever visited on Earth. That's not really saying a whole hell of a lot, because I never traveled too far from my South Georgia home.

I've read about Renaissance fairs, though, and the other women tell me this is as close to a Ren-Fest as it gets. That is if the Ren-Fests on Earth had been running daily for hundreds of years, covered thousands of acres, and were a destination tourist attraction from all over the galaxy.

Just like on Earth, people are encouraged to wear the garb of their ancestors. It still has dirt pathways and old-fashioned booths made of wood and emblazoned with fabric. Electronics are frowned upon except for the computerized maps people are given when they enter the park.

Just walking through the fair is a delight to the senses. From the dozens of alien species to the thousands of booths to the foreign food smells—this place delights me.

It's not just the random sights, smells, and tastes that enchant me; for the past two months I've walked by a certain someone's booth every time I'm here. And since my very first day, a certain someone always manages to be leaning casually in his doorway when I travel past him on the dusty path.

He's handsome, in an alien way. I've always been attracted to the bad boys. There was a string of them in high school until one by one they all dropped out. After I graduated and my parents passed away, I was too busy keeping the farm operation going to care much about any man. No matter if he was good or bad, he'd be a distraction from my little farm.

I called him Leather Man in my head for the first few weeks, then we properly introduced ourselves. Revikk doesn't seem all that different from the boys I used to date. That is if you can overlook the blue skin and patterned ridges and blue eyes that burn so brightly they almost glow. There's something brash in the way he looks at me. He makes no secret of what he'd like to do with me. He doesn't sneak glances at my breasts. No, his gaze lingers on them so long it's impertinent.

And truth be told, I like it.

What can I say? When I'm around him I feel a sensual yearning deep in my belly. I haven't felt that in a long, time. What would be wrong with sharing a moment with him in the wooden structure behind the tented overhang where he sells his handmade leather goods?

I sashay past his booth with just the right swing in my step, hoping when he gets a view of my rear, he likes my wiggle. After I make my egg delivery five doors down, I mosey back to his booth and strike up a conversation just like I have for months.

Before I can say anything, he drawls, "Hi, Miss Dawn."

He's always very polite with his words, even as his blue eyes slide up and down my body, stopping at his favorite parts.

"Hi, Revikk." I bite back my urge to playfully ask him how it's hanging. My momma, God rest her soul, raised me better than that.

We make the usual small talk as I take his inventory for the hundredth time. Wide shoulders, trim hips, and not an ounce of fat. He's one big tall male made of sheer muscle. His alien face with those attractive angular grooves is handsome, there's no denying that, but it's his self-assurance that attracts me even more.

He stands in that brown fringed suede jacket he wears over leather pants that have a . . . what was it I learned when we studied Shakespeare in high school? A hard leather codpiece. How does he expect a female's eyes not to arrow right in on that piece of equipment? One has to but glance at it to begin wondering what's behind it.

He's smirking at me. He knows right where I was looking and exactly what I was thinking. Sorry, not sorry that he caught me.

That smirk. On a million other males it would make me want to wipe it off their smug faces. On Revikk? I want to kiss those self-satisfied lips.

The big blue male's posture screams nonchalance while his piercing blue eyes scream interest—sexual interest.

"We've been talking for weeks now," I say coquettishly with a toss of my shoulder-length blond hair, "and you've yet to show me where the magic happens." I glance meaningfully through his doorway, pause, then add, "Where you make your art."

His mouth tips into a lopsided smile.

"*Art*, huh?"

His leatherwork *is* artistic. He has some large pieces, the perfect size to hang over a couch, that are hand stamped in intricate patterns, then dyed. Some are abstract, some are realistic landscapes or animal scenes.

But we both know what I'm really referring to.

"Speaking of my art, I have a small present for you." His smirk wavers for a moment, revealing just a smidgeon of apprehension that I might not appreciate his gift. His moment of bashful vulnerability is surprising and endearing.

"A present?" I should shut up. I'm a private person, I don't share a lot of myself with others—even the guy I think I'll be exchanging bodily fluids with in a few minutes. But I offer, "I haven't received a present in a long time," my voice gets that dreamy tone, and my eyes look off into the distance at nothing.

"After my folks died, my last two birthdays were present-less. And since my abduction . . ." I shrug and realize that if he's looking closely, he'll see my eyes are shining a bit too brightly.

"Then all the more reason to enjoy this." He slips into his back room and returns with a purse dangling off the crook of one finger.

It looks like the softest doeskin I've ever seen. The light creamy yellow is delicate and natural. My fingers itch to take it, touch it, examine it, but I wait, my muscles coiled in anticipation, for him to hand it to me.

"Here." No smirk now as he gifts it to me with both hands. Somehow, the gesture seems more meaningful that way.

"Ohh." I was right. This thing is softer than almost anything I've ever touched. "Lovely."

It's about the size of a spiral notebook and built more for show than utility. The strap is thin, but thick enough I'll never worry it will break. Although the stitching is perfect, the flap is artfully asymmetrical and a bit rugged in a way that screams it was handmade—one of a kind. The closure is made of a knobby button made of horn that slips into a leather loop.

"I love it."

My tummy feels all swirly. Maybe it was the swift, unexpected memories of my deceased parents, or perhaps it was receiving a gift. Feeling, even for a moment, that he thought of me while creating it makes me feel a warmth inside I haven't experienced in a long time. The bag is unlike anything hanging in the front of the booth. It's one-of-a-kind. Made for me.

But the swirlies in my stomach kick into overdrive when I look up at him and see a look of approval on his face. His perma-sneer is gone for once and he looks genuinely pleased with my appreciation of his gift.

"Love it?" He tilts his head, challenging me as if my praise was insincere.

"I'll cherish it." Yeah Revikk, I doubled down.

"You wanted to see where the magic happens?" he manages to ask without sounding lecherous.

A moment later, I've followed him into his dim living quarters. It's maybe ten feet wide and fifteen feet long. The front half is an explosion of tools and leather scraps and works in progress with two workbenches, one on each long wall.

In the back is his living space which is almost spartan. A well-made bed, wide enough for two, a dresser, a table, and two chairs. Weak light filters in from dusty skylights. Because he keeps his personal half neat, the space doesn't seem cluttered.

I feel like the fly to his spider as he gives me a tour of a worktable and shows me a few projects in progress even as he keeps inching toward the private part of his space, the highlight of which is the bed.

"That concludes the tour," he says, then he spears me with his electric blue gaze and waits expectantly.

I realize he's not going to ask me to join him in bed, not out loud anyway. His mouth tips into that lazy, crooked smile again and he just waits as if he has all the time in the world.

Although I had every intention of doing the deed with him today, I suddenly feel like a deer caught in the headlights.
"You said you live in a compound. Are there other males there?" he prompts.

I nod, then add, "They're all gladiators."

"Do you have a mate?"

"No."

"A bedmate then?" his voice lowered even as one eyebrow winged up in question.

"No." My eyes sneak to his bed. It's as bold a statement as I can make. I guess I'm not as forward as I thought I was.

"Would you like to join me?" He tips his chin toward the quilt-covered bed.

"Yes!" I answer in a rush, glad he finally asked.

Revikk, Mr. Nonchalance, goes from calm and still as a tree to immediate action. He crosses the room and presses a button just inside the door.

"I activated the autozip closures. The booth is closed," his voice is deep, level.

Then he covers the space between us in three large steps, puts his palms on my upper arms, and nips my neck. It shocks me even as it sends a hot, almost electric charge through my body.

He scrapes his teeth on the cords of my neck and flicks my earlobe with the tip of his tongue. He grabs my hair lightly and tips my head back so he can nibble along my jawbone from one ear to the other.

I thought we'd start with kisses, but there isn't a kiss in sight. Instead, it's an onslaught, an assault that steals my breath.

It's as if I've been waiting for this my entire life. It's fire and ice and everything in between. He positions himself so that his hard leather codpiece presses into the 'v' between my legs and he mimics sex right here while we're still standing near his workbench. His pelvis thrusts and grinds in an interesting rhythm made more interesting by the fact I'm bent over backward with my clit ripe for the taking.

He was like a snake just waiting to uncoil and strike with swift ferocity.

"I'm going to *drack* you, Dawn. I'm going to do all the things I've been thinking about since the first time I met you. I want to find out if you're a screamer or a moaner or one of those rare females who take their pleasure silently.

"I'm going to figure out if your breasts fit perfectly in the palm of my hand and if your cream is sweet or spicy. I'm not going to stop until I've had my fill or you tell me to stop. Do you understand?"

By the end of his soliloquy, he's peeled us apart and is standing an inch from me, his face at my level. His eyes are punctuating his statements by piercing me with a gaze so fiery, so sincere, they demand an answer.

"Yes."

His lips twitch in a satisfied smirk I have little time to notice because he bends to remove his clothes. When he realizes I'm not moving he says, "Want to do it fully clothed? You still have to remove your . . ."

His facile hand grabs me above the knee and slides up my thigh to my crotch. There's no artifice, this move wasn't meant to arouse, he's on a recon mission. When his fingers encounter my lacey pink panties, I dressed for the occasion, he barks, "Panties!"

Startled into action, I pull off my panties, then realize that was a command of last resort. What we both really want is for me to be naked. I rip the pretty, swingy floral summer dress over my head and stand in front of him naked.

Was he waiting for me to strip, because he's taking his time. He already removed his thin suede shirt, exposing his rippled abs. The sexy grooves that add definition to his face also decorate his chest. As if his body wasn't magnificent enough, the grooves pull my gaze like a magnet.

He pulls off his pants, which are kind of like cowboy chaps, although unlike the kind we have on earth, they cover his ass. They split in the front, though, so the codpiece can bulge out, taking center stage.

That's the only piece of clothing he's wearing, and by the look of it, he was waiting for the unveiling until he got my full attention. I watch, making no secret I'm excitedly awaiting his big reveal. Holy shit! The word 'big' was certainly descriptive.

His hand darts to my wrist and he drags me to the wall, not-so-gently pressing my front against it. This building, little more than a shed with a door, was constructed of wooden boards long ago. It's rough and ancient, and the force with which I was tossed against it turns me on.

This is nothing like the few adolescent fumblings I shared in the back of my Georgia boyfriends' cars. No, Revikk is full of well-controlled power, and by the drenched state of the panties I just removed, he's using it for good, not evil.

The wood is coarse against my already-pebbled nipples; his palms are possessive as they slide from my shoulders to my hips. Turning my head to look at him over my shoulder, I watch the molten desire in his eyes as he takes me in, gets accustomed to the feel of me, seems to memorize every hill and valley of my curves.

"Soft," he says in a quiet huff.

Both hands slide down my hips, his thumbs reaching toward the crevice of my ass. No Georgia boys ever ventured here, yet it's his first move. Instead of repulsing me, I quiver in anticipation.

One thumb breaches the line, teases up and down the crack without touching me there. The wood feels scratchy on my cheek as I reposition to get a better look at him.

"I'm a possessive male," he enunciates each word carefully. "I want to own every part of you. I'll stop whenever you say. This . . ." His thumb breaches the invisible line, circles my tight pucker, and moves back to my cheek. "This will come later."

I was sopping wet before I received my present. Just talking to him gets me excited. Being invited to his private sanctum, tearing off my clothes, watching him expose that alarmingly beautiful cock, I'm dripping wet. This? All my preconceptions to the contrary, this catapulted me into being ablaze with desire.

Lifting me by the waist, he sets me an inch away from the wall so his hands can plunder up over my ribcage and cup my breasts. He hisses in pleasure, pumps that monster between his legs against my ass, and says, "Yes, a nice handful."

His appreciation pleases me.

"And you're dripping for me," he says, although he hasn't explored between my legs to be able to make that statement with certainty.

He bites my earlobe, thrusts against my backside, and plucks both nipples at the same time. I'm already moaning in response to his actions.

"Oh, Dawn, I'm betting you're a moaner *and* a screamer. My favorite."

Although none of my previous boyfriends pulled a moan *or* a scream from me, I have no doubt Revikk's guess is going to be correct.

"Legs apart." The words are an order, but his tone is warm honey on a summer day.

My compliance is greeted with his command, "Wider."

"Mmm, that's right. Open wide for me."

His hand slides slowly down from where it was tantalizing my hardened nipple and pauses a moment, his fingers pointing toward one hipbone and the heel of his hand toward the other.

"Tell me how much you want me."

I like this position. My cheek against the rough wooden wall, I'm facing away from him, his teeth are nipping the cords on the other side of my neck. He can't see my expressions. It's freeing.

"I want you." My voice sounds so breathy, so unlike me when I'm calling my little *prens* from the other side of their pen.

"More, Dawn," he coaxes, his hand tracing a two-inch swath up and down from hipbones to mons and back again. He's withholding until I cough up more words.

"I want your hand on me." Shit! I wanted this so much, but I'm still shy.

"My hand is on you, Dawn. Tell me *where*." His low tone is so persuasive—dirty little nothings come so easily to his lips.

"I want your hand between my legs." To emphasize my request, I widen my stance.

It's only when he cups me between my legs so lightly it's as if he's not even touching me that I realize Revikk is a sadist.

"Like this?" he goads sweetly.

He's going to force me to talk dirty.

"Slide your finger inside me."

"You're almost there, little Dawn. Say my name and you'll get what you want."

"Put your finger inside me, Revikk."

His finger moves so slowly it's like molten lava as it moves to my mons, then slides through my slick folds toward my core. His touch is soft, not like the possessive frenzy he displayed earlier, but it makes me tremble with desire.

One long, thick finger slips into me with unhurried patience. As I feel every inch of him, I release a high little moan, more like a whimper. Then, quick as a wink, he pulls out and my channel is empty. This simple act makes me *ache* in loneliness.

"Is that what you wanted?" he goads.

"No."

"Tell me."

It strikes me like a thunderbolt that talk is this male's foreplay.

I drag in a deep breath, give myself a silent push, and jump off the cliff.

"Revikk, I want your finger pumping into me until I squirm with pleasure, then I want you to follow it with a second and perhaps a third. I want the heel of your hand on my clit circling while you do that until I come apart with a moan and a scream."

That wasn't so hard! It was fun!

"Then I want—"

"What is a clit?" he interrupts me with a tone lacking honey. It's urgent and demanding.

"It's what makes a female come. How do other species do it?"

"Show me," he insists. "Take my finger."

When I grab the finger he's extended near my core, I give him a guided tour, not skimping on the narration.

"This little lump of flesh. It's a bundle of nerves. It's so sensitive that you have to work around it like this." I circle myself like I do in bed at night.

He thrusts against my back in a lusty rhythm. "Do it, Dawn. Bring yourself release with my finger. You'll never have to show me again."

Of that, I have no doubt.

He nips the cords of my neck, then my earlobe, then plucks a nipple with his free hand, still thrusting against me from behind.

"Show me," he urges.

I dip his finger in my core to moisten it although it's already slippery, drag it to my clit, then get to work.

"That's right," he encourages when my breathing hitches.

I press harder, circle faster, and suddenly my muscles clench, my knees sag, and I come with a long moan.

His other arm has migrated to my waist and is holding me up as I pant.

"I get it," he reassures me. "That's the end of the tutorial. Don't worry that you only gave yourself a moan. I'll have you screaming before too long."

My torso is still pressed against the wall, my ass jacked back to allow for all the action. Revikk gives me a moment to recover as he kisses my neck, ear, and hair, then he begins playing with his new toy.

I have to give him credit, he follows directions to a T. He begins by pressing one finger deep into me, and then a second. His rhythm mimics what I was doing to myself.

I'm panting like a racehorse, wiggling my tush against him, and making little mewling sounds.
"
Ask for it," he urges.

"Make me come, Revikk."

The heel of his hand circles me. He's quiet, listening to my tells. How ragged I'm breathing, how hard I push against him, my sighs. He makes minor adjustments as if he's living in my head. Pleasuring me better than I can pleasure myself.

My body's ramped up, poised on the edge of release. I know the ticket to paradise—I have to speak.

"Make me come, Revikk. Harder."

He bites my neck with the flat of his teeth, not enough to draw blood, just enough to burn. At the same time, the heel of his hand presses harder and a third finger joins the other two. My orgasm gallops in, picking up speed and then running away with me as every muscle in my body clenches.

I'm not trying to please him by making the noises that are escaping my mouth; they're coming of their own accord. Deep, feral moans from the back of my throat are capped off by a swift scream of pleasure as my muscles seize up in intense rolling waves of ecstasy.

Buy Revikk on Amazon. He'll be available in Kindle Unlimited.

Glossary

Drack—the perfect all-purpose expletive. It's a noun, it's a verb, it's an adjective.

Fairea—FAIR-ee-uh

Fierto—foot

Hoara—hour

Ince—inch

mille—mile

Minima—minute

Modicum—second

Lunar or lunar cycle—month

Rextan—acre

Galaxy Gladiators Alien Abduction Romance Series

Zar

Shadow

Tyree

Devolose

Drayke

Axxios & Braxxus

Jax-Xon

Sirius

Dax

Beast

Ar'Tok

Wrage

WarDog

Stryker

Vartan

Galaxy Pirates Alien Abduction Romance Series

Sextus

Thantose

Ssly

Slag

Galaxy Sanctuary Alien Abduction Romance Series

Thran

Abraxx

Revikk

Mastered by the Zinn Alien Abduction Romance Series

Voxx 1

Voxx 2

Voxx 3

Treasured by the Zinn Alien Abduction Romance Series

Arzz

Trev

Sinn

Men of Blackstone

Direct Me

Heal Me

Instruct Me

Teach Me

BOX SETS

Box Set - Galaxy Gladiators Alien Abduction Romance
Series Books 1 to 3

Box Set - Galaxy Gladiators Alien Abduction Romance
Series Books 1 to 4

Box Set - First In Series - Zar / Sextus / Arzz

Box Set - Treasured by the Zinn Alien Abduction Romance
Series

Box Set - Mastered by the Zinn Alien Abduction Romance
Series